BACKSTOP

A NOVEL

DAVIS FALK

Published by Red Shirt Books

First (paperback/ Ebook) edition 2023

Paperback ISBN: 979-8-9877155-0-5
Hardback ISBN: 979-8-9877155-1-2
eBook ISBN: 979-8-9877155-2-9

Cover art and interior layout by MiblArt

CONTENTS

CHAPTER ONE

FAR AWAY

At first, the only sound was of the whining engines and rushing air of a jet flying over. Next came an unbelievable cacophony as several floors of glass windows shattered. The impact was so rapid that the twisting steel girders didn't creak so much as they screamed in agony. Deadly asbestos dust filled the air as all of the insulation was ripped to shreds. Aluminum crumpled like a soft drink can, plastic crackled, and seats were torn from their mounts all over what, seconds earlier, was the intact body of the Boeing 767 airliner. No trace of its original shape remained. A fireball erupted from the northern face of the North Tower of the World Trade Center as 10,000 gallons of aviation fuel burst from the aircraft's wing tanks. Floors ninety-three through ninety-nine erupted in flames as jet fuel ignited, incinerating paper, furniture, paintings, and carpeting. The 400-degree heatwave boiled all liquid in its path and melted what it didn't burn as it spread in all directions. Everyone on the plane and on those floors was killed either by the impact or the subsequent inferno.

In her Toronto apartment, a black-haired, thirtyish woman sat staring at her television screen as the local station replayed the ten-year-old video of the September 11, 2001 crash of American Airlines Flight 11. A news anchor continued her narration: "In the streets below, panic ensued as the debris fell and the ground literally shook from the impact…"

The watching woman's calm, stone-cold countenance belied a secret hidden deep within her mind. Her eyes were glazed over. Softly she sang, "Somewhere, over the rainbow…"

CHAPTER TWO

SEPTEMBER 11, 2001

Midnight. Still wearing the flight attendant's uniform she had put on 18 hours earlier, Julie sat facing a tired-looking, slim man, probably about her age, she guessed. The room was large, with a high ceiling. The floor was grey tile—the kind you see in grocery stores and laundromats. It was cold enough to be slightly uncomfortable. Along one wall were a sink, microwave, and coffee machines. Modern stuffed chairs and coffee tables littered the room in a random pattern. It looked like a makeshift lounge for crew or workers passing through the facility. No one else was in the room.

No one else was in the room except Julie and the young man sitting across from her, wearing a jacket and shirt with no tie. He looked like a politician trying to appear casual without giving up the air of authority. He was scanning a document of several stapled-together pages as if studying for a speech. She had been separated from the other passengers and crew from her flight and hadn't seen any of them for a couple of hours. Like most people, she trusted that things would generally be okay. But the hours of waiting, the unknown had made her increasingly anxious, and she felt a vague fear lurking in the back corners of her mind.

A little tired as well, Julie ran her hands through her jet-black pixie-cut hair. She rested one arm across her knees, the other hand supporting her chin and brushing back and forth across her full lips. She was glad she had worn pants. The building was quite cool, wherever it was. Her flying instincts told her it was probably Cleveland or Indianapolis. Definitely not Chicago.

"You should be fine," he said, with a little too much emphasis on the word *should*. "You understand; it's National Security. Unfortunately, we won't be able to help you after today. But you seem to be resourceful." He fumbled for a stapled set of pages. "You'll need to read this and sign it," he said, handing her the document. "There are some rules."

CHAPTER THREE

TEN YEARS LATER

t was a dead end.

"It's not a dead end," Jacob said into his phone.

"What have you got? After all this work and time, what have we got? What have you got?" asked Andreas. Jacob imagined his frustrated older partner sitting in a bookshelf-lined study in his Virginia home.

Jacob stood up from the desk in his Manhattan studio apartment. His chocolate-brown eyes darted around him as if he was taking a quick inventory.

"We have the videos, the engineering, the lack of government claims, and the wrongful death suits," said Jacob. He tried to be convincing. Andreas was the most intelligent guy he knew, but he did not have that passionate optimism so necessary in investigative journalism. His academic skepticism was helpful at times. He never accepted the quick assumptions Jacob was sometimes willing to make. But Andreas's skepticism could also be paralyzing. "Look, Andreas, you are the authority on passenger manifest anomalies. We need you in the fight. You've done a lot, and there's more work to be done. You can't just give up. There's too much at stake."

Andreas sighed.

"I tell you what," Jacob offered, "take the weekend and get away from all this. We'll dig in more next week. Take more time if you need it. Step away and recharge your batteries. Meantime, I'll keep working."

"Okay, but what is there to work on?" The older man chuckled.

"There's a sort of convention coming up, first of its kind. 'TruthCon' up in Boston. Anyone interested or involved in The Movement is invited. Discussion panels, vendor booths, seminars, mixers—it's full service! I'm going to nose around and see what others have done that isn't public yet."

After disconnecting from his call with Andreas, Jacob sat down. His hair color matched the color of his eyes. His dark features made him look Asian or Native American, though he had no idea of his ancestry. He was near average height with a lean build.

Jacob turned back to his computer and found the website for "TruthCon." It showed pictures of authors famous for their writings on various aspects of the events surrounding the 9/11 attacks. Beside each image was a paragraph describing the life and works of the man or woman pictured. One picture was of a distinguished-looking man in a tweed jacket whose expertise was the strategic and geopolitical motives that might have led to the 9/11 attacks and others. Another picture showed a smiling, clean-cut man in horn-rimmed glasses and thin, dark hair who was a member of Architects and Engineers for 9/11 Truth. A wry smile came over Jacob's face as he imagined Andreas' face there. Andreas had spent years investigating and researching the theory that passengers initially manifested on the wrecked flights had been diverted, killed, or never got on those flights.

It was early, and Jacob was sipping his morning coffee. A large L-shaped desk, cluttered with digital cameras, tripods, notebooks, and a small laptop, consumed half of the tiny living space. The equipment had scratches, areas of missing paint, and minor repairs, the signs of heavy field use. In a corner near the desk were boxes of t-shirts and baseball caps with various conspiracy-theory slogans on them along with his website address. He had to go to work. He clicked the "Sign Up Now!" button and entered his information, then put on a jacket that had been thrown over the back of his office chair, grabbed his keys off a hook near the kitchen area, and walked out the door of the apartment.

CHAPTER FOUR

ROAD TRIP

Steve walked up to the counter and gave the cashier a stupid look. "You got any good driving beers?" The middle-aged cashier smiled and shook his head as if to say, "kids these days..." Jacob laughed as he walked up behind him and slammed a large can of Rock Star on the counter.

"We're not in Canada yet, dude. Are you even old enough to drink here?" He paid for the energy drink and some snacks, and they walked out the door of the convenience store together.

"Uh, yeah, unless they raised it to 25. I'm younger than you, but not that young." Steve got in the passenger side of his red 2002 Honda Civic as Jacob slid in behind the wheel, finding a place for his speed-in-a-can somewhere in the console between the front seats. "But I'm not taking this trip to get drunk. Okay, maybe a little bit. It's more about the talent, though."

"Right, I almost forgot. Talent. Very important. The talent is much better north of the border." They were headed for the Toronto nightlife, famous, at least in some circles, for strip clubs that are much more liberal and "hands-on" than any such establishment in New England or, in fact, anywhere in the states. Though it had become a sort of ritual with the two old friends, Jacob was beginning to outgrow it. But he didn't get to see Steve that often, and they couldn't think of anything else to do. "I'm surprised Michaelyn let you go on this little jaunt."

"Oh, you don't know her; she's cool as all get out. Man, I still can't believe you missed my bachelor party. Talk about talent!" Steve had been married for three years. Jacob had met Michaelyn but hadn't spent much time with either of them during that time.

"I was busy attending the premiere of *Freefall 2*."

Jacob had come to Boston for the convention, and spending time with his old friend was an added benefit. Steve and Michaelyn were allowing him to sleep on their couch in between the scheduled activities, mixers, and the private meetings he was able to set up with fellow serious researchers. It seemed he was taking advantage, so when Steve suggested the traditional Toronto road trip, he had little choice but to go along.

They were already several hours down the Masspike, the local name for Interstate 90, which runs from downtown Boston to Buffalo, New York, and into the Midwest. They would be stopping in Rochester for a high-speed ferry to Toronto. It was mid-fall now, not quite leaf-peeping season and unusually sunny. The Interstate was lined with thick green trees. Jacob sipped on his Rock Star, wearing a black FDNY t-shirt over his jeans. As always, the backpack he carried, now in the back seat, held at least one digital camera, just in case something relevant caught his eye. He was relaxed and enjoying his leisure, but a part of his mind was still on his work and eager to act on the new information he had found at *TruthCon*.

CHAPTER FIVE

TRUTHCON

TRUTHCON.NET

About TruthCon

In the ten years since the 9/11 attacks, an entire field of study has developed. A dozen universities in the United States have at least one course related to this event. One even has a program leading to a certificate. Outside of academia, scores of authors, journalists, forensic investigators, and historians have taken up the study of the events and the impact of this one day as a full- or part-time avocation. Hundreds of theories have developed as to the how's and the why's. Researchers use minutiae extracted from airport security videos to support the idea that the alleged hijackers never boarded the airplanes. Engineers have used massive experiments in explosives and aviation accidents to debate whether or not a wide-body jet struck the Pentagon or how the fire in the World Trade Center buildings could cause the building to collapse so quickly. Everyone asks one question: Why? Military and security training on the subject of airliners crashed into buildings, some from decades before, have been uncovered to ask whether this type of attack was unexpected. A TV drama using the same plot aired only months before the attacks – did it give the terrorists the idea? Communications engineers and air traffic controllers have been interviewed to determine how passengers and crew used cellular phones to make calls from Flight 93 if the aircraft was so high as to be out of range of cellular towers. Each of these areas has many investigators, bloggers, and media figures who argue the fine points and theorized conclusions.

The Wild West of 9/11 research and commentary concerns the mysterious: the unknown facts, gaps in information which invite the imagination to enter by way of explanation. The human mind seeks order in the world and meaning in its timeline. Every traumatic event demands a reason. Thus, the practice of describing these events as tragic. Tragedy is a form of theatrical writing in which the protagonist possesses a fatal flaw that eventually leads to his undoing. Romeo's impulsiveness leads to his death by premature suicide. There is no shortage of people willing to write the tragic story leading up to the events of September 11, 2001. All of the gaps and mysteries still in existence are used as opportunities to provide supporting narrative "facts." From the sinister to the corrupt, from the zealous to the fanatical, a universe of theoretical actors and motives behind the crime has emerged. Historical acts of violence and treachery support these real or imagined villains' and cabals' assumed purpose and existence. Having established the history, proponents of these theories can blame these supposed puppeteers for any future action. There is no limit to the expansion of the myth.

At TruthCon.net, *we have learned through long experience to differentiate between the fantasy writers and the hard-nosed investigators in the field of 9/11 investigation. Both are always looking for disciples and stringers to recruit to their cause. We sympathize with those trying to find a grand solution, but we only support purely fact-based work.*

TruthCon, *as its name indicates, center on finding the truth about 9/11. The organizers here at* TruthCon. net *doubt the "official story" and are partial to alternative explanations. However, we invite and accept presenters with all manner of investigatory findings and ongoing narratives. Activist organizations seeking to right the wrongs against victims, families, first responders, and others and to change how things are done in the future are also welcome. We seek the truth. If you feel the same way,* TruthCon *may be for you.*

A steady afternoon rain fell, typical of Boston in October, and nowhere near enough to stop the determined pedestrians moving out of Back Bay Station. Most dressed in dark colors from head to toe, many with hats worn against the wet, windy chill, and all pleased it was still rain and not yet snow. Business at the Starbucks on Dartmouth Street was booming. Jacob had to wait ten minutes for his venti triple mocha, well worth it, as he braved the slosh once again and moved with the crowd toward Copley Square. It was Friday morning, and not much would be going on at Copley Plaza in the way of convention events, other than early registration and some setup activities. But Jacob knew many attendees and presenters would already be around. He would meet up with people he knew or get to know people he met. He had emailed Ty, one of the old *Freefall* gang who was still involved in the franchise. They didn't have anything new out but would have a booth where they would sell *Freefall* and *Freefall 2* DVDs and T-shirts, sign autographs, answer questions, and gather addresses for their email list. Jacob slowed down and took a long drink of his coffee, now just cool enough to drink without burning his tongue. As the chocolate, caffeine, and warm milk went down, warming and invigorating his body, he stood on the corner of Dartmouth and St. James streets admiring the gothic edifice of the Boston Public Library. Its vast front sidewalk seemed out of place in the crowded streets of Back Bay, amidst the humming tracks of the inbound trains and the morning traffic running through the Prudential Tunnel. Satisfied, he continued down St. James toward the hotel.

The Fairmont Copley Plaza Hotel was built in 1912, the same year as Fenway Park. Its décor was of an era when luxury and wealth were not understated, and the fancier and more lavish, the better. Jacob walked in and took in the high ceilings and ornamentation as he shook off the rain. Involuntarily, he relaxed the shoulders he had hunched in the weather as he walked the three long blocks from the train station. He looked around the spacious lobby where a few people were sitting in big leather overstuffed chairs. He didn't notice anyone he knew, so he decided to give Ty a call. Ty answered his call and said he'd be right down. Jacob put down his backpack, sat in one of the leather chairs, and sipped his coffee. While he waited, he glanced at the headlines of a *Boston Globe* that lay on a nearby table—more bad news about the Worldwide Economy. He figured there might be something about the convention in one of the weekend editions, or Monday's, unless something more important happened, like another country's government going bankrupt.

"Wassup!" Ty walked up and slapped hands with Jacob. "Let's go to the restaurant. Have you eaten yet? I'm starving.'" He spoke with a strong Brooklyn accent and wore black jeans and a black t-shirt with "911 Was an Inside Job" in white letters. The two 1's in 911 were styled to look like the twin towers of the World Trade Center.

Ty was tall, lanky, but muscular enough not to be skinny, with a messy blond mop of hair. The quieter, more passive of the four *Freefall* producers played an essential role as a loyal and fearless supporter and advocate. He wasn't afraid to speak out, though. Jacob recalled several rather loud arguments between Ty and others in the group, especially about military members and veterans. Like Jacob, Ty's father had served in the Gulf War.

Breakfast came, and Ty's eyes started to open as they ate, and he sipped a second cup of coffee.

"So what's next for you guys?" asked Jacob.

"Dunno, Jake," Ty started. "Feedback is kind of fractured, you know. After the first one, they all asked for more. We gave it to them in the second one. Now, it's like everybody wants us to go into some niche area. But those movies have already been done. So we're lookin' for a new project. But I don't want to do another one just 'cause that's the next thing to do, you know."

"Yeah. You gotta keep your integrity, or you lose credibility," said Jacob.

"So we've been doing some radio. I think there might be a market for a regular gig on satellite, but it would be more than 9/11. We'd have to get into more stuff. But what's going on now is all related, so maybe that would work. So what about you? Is Andreas coming?" Ty motioned for more coffee as the waiter took his breakfast plate away.

"Nah," replied Jacob. "He'd never show up at one of these things. He's not a people person. Andreas prefers microfilm, newsprint, the occasional magazine. He spends a lot of time on the phone."

"I guess that's why you two make such a good team," said Ty, "you being the 'combat photographer' and all."

"I guess so. Speaking of which," Jacob deftly pulled his Nikon out of his backpack and had the lens cap off, and the camera focused on Ty's face. It happened all in one motion, with the grace of a seasoned photographer. He scanned the background as he shot three bracketed exposures, a habit he'd picked up trying to capture those that didn't want to be captured.

"We're getting stuck now," Jacob said. "Not much information coming in. I was hoping to meet some people here that we haven't seen online, maybe share some info." Jacob put his camera down and looked out the window as a ray of sunlight came through the clouds.

"Did you ever get that guy in Cleveland on record?" Ty's question referred to reports of a flight that landed in Cleveland on the morning of September 11th at about 10:10 a.m. The pilot was concerned that a bomb was on board, and the airplane was quarantined and evacuated. The "guy" was Cleveland Mayor Michael White.

"He still won't talk to us," Jacob grumbled, "but I haven't actually gone there yet."

"Yeah," said Ty. "It's amazing how some people will never even take your call, then when you show up at their office or home, they invite you in for coffee!" The two friends laughed at the irony that they knew from experience was the truth.

"So that's probably my next trip if I come up dry here," said Jacob, nodding. "Is this thing gonna be any good?"

"We'll see. It's the first official one by the Truth guys. The other ones have been kind of thrown-together events at little towns, and maybe a hundred people showed up. This one should be bigger, though," Ty said as his eyes got slightly wider.

"Because it's here?" Jacob asked.

"No. They have David Icke as the keynote speaker." Ty's face betrayed a grain-of-salt look.

"The shape-shifting lizard guy?" Jacob smiled and almost laughed. "It's been a while since his 9/11 book came out."

"He was available," Ty said with a shrug, "and he can fill a room with 2000 people. I think they wanted to ensure they wouldn't lose money on the first event, especially being held at a place like this," Ty motioned with his hand at the gold-leaf sconces and towering drapes, the opulence all around them. "He's hotter now than ever, actually. Not sure why."

"Well," Jacob said, "more people doesn't make it a good turnout for me—not if it's just the lunatic fringe that shows up."

The check came, and Ty signed for it to be charged to his room. "I have to set up the booth by noon," Ty said. "If you want to help out, I'll show you our video from the 10th anniversary. I haven't seen yours either." Jacob agreed, and they stood up to leave. The grand ballroom was where all the booths were being set up. Hanging out there was probably the best chance to meet the people he wanted to meet.

Later, after the evening speaker, Ty and Josh Aidan, another of the *Freefall* producers, closed their booth. Along with Jacob and a pair of passenger researchers they had met that afternoon, they retired to Legal Sea Foods down the street for a late dinner. Josh was all business and did a lot of the talking.

"So what do you guys plan to do with this, Jake?" Josh was another New Yorker whose day job was working in a corporate IT department before *Freefall* allowed him to turn pro as a filmmaker. But it wasn't like making Hollywood movies. If he and Ty didn't find a project soon that would pay, they would be forced to go back to their day jobs and wouldn't have any working capital left either.

"We don't have enough information to do anything now," Jacob replied, "but the assumption is that if we do find something, Andreas will write a book, and I'll make a film, and we'll both contribute to both projects." Jacob knew Josh could get excited about a project and liked to be busy.

Josh looked at Ty. "Maybe we should get in on this. It's the kind of thing that sucks people in. Very intriguing."

"I'm telling you, there's no point now," Jacob stated. "There's a huge hole in the theory that's keeping us from seeing the big picture. When we did *Freefall*, we were investigating events witnessed by millions of people, and most of the material we needed was all in NYC. All we have now is a bunch of unrelated anomalies that could just be misunderstandings and miscommunication." Jacob looked at Ty and then at Josh with understanding and regret about their situation. Then he looked down at his surf-n-turf, barely touched since it arrived ten minutes ago, picked up his steak knife, and began to work on the meat. "I think it's time we heard from our new friends, though. Maybe they can change all that," he said, looking to his right expectantly.

John Thompson was a local, a retired Smith & Wesson gunsmith from Springfield. His hair was short but not quite military. He wore wire-rimmed glasses and a plaid shirt. Every word he spoke was accompanied by a gesture, usually involving both hands. One got the feeling he was also gesturing with his feet as if still working the machine tools he had used most of his life.

"What got me interested," Thompson began, "was a local story that somehow got missed by the networks. It was about a security guard at Logan." Thompson scooted his chair closer to the table. "It seems he had been asked to usher a group of people who had already boarded a plane into an empty customs storage area."

"I can't believe it," Jacob said. Thompson looked over at him, more surprised than annoyed at the interruption. "I've searched every video that exists on that day, especially in Boston. I haven't seen that." This statement was almost true. Jacob was nothing if not persistent and thorough, and he had personally contacted every TV station in Boston, New York, DC, and Shanksville.

"It wasn't on TV," said Thompson, "and it's never been online." To the layman, especially people under the age of twenty, this might have seemed absurd. But Jacob knew that in 2001, most TV video, even news footage, was not available online. Fewer people had broadband internet service. There was no YouTube. Thompson continued. "The guy was a commuter from Springfield. After his shift, he had time to think during his drive home. Then he called a local radio DJ he knew who convinced him to do a live interview. There was a small piece in the Springfield Union-News, as well. I can send it to you."

"Did you talk to him?" Josh asked.

"No," Thompson replied. "At the time, it seemed like he had said all he knew to the DJ—Bob Kessler."

"Could you talk to him now?" Josh was still very interested in this idea, especially if the story had loose ends that needed bird-dogging. "I'm sure he'd remember a lot."

"Nope," said a new voice. This time John's companion, a fellow Springfielder, spoke up. He didn't use his hands at all and kept them folded over his ample belly when they weren't gathering lobster and French fries from his plate. "Dead. Heart attack in 2004." He spoke like one of the Kennedys, the short "a" with no "r" in "heart attack" coming from somewhere in the back of his throat.

"Nobody interviewed him after that," continued Thompson. "You could get a hold of Kessler, but I doubt he would provide anything new."

"So, what do you have?" Jacob wondered if the first day of the convention was turning into a bust.

"No, no, no. That's just the beginning," said John's friend, whose name was Pete Rodolpho. "We're talking about a ghost flight. We've been working this angle since day one."

"Ghost flight?" Now, Ty was intrigued.

CHAPTER SIX

THE SIGHTING

"What are we doing? Where are we going?" Steve was trying to keep up with Jacob while having a conversation and weaving through rush-hour pedestrian traffic down Wellington Street.

"Breakfast. Gretzky's," Jacob replied, alert and ready to move. They had been out the night before and had a few drinks. But Jacob had quit early. He also drank plenty of water and took enough Advil to be completely hangover-free. Coffee in the hotel room had helped, and some food would complete the course of treatment. He was a man on a mission for donuts.

"But all they have is donuts," said Steve. "Let's go to Denny's and get some protein."

"There's no Denny's here. I thought you liked Gretzky's." Jacob adjusted his backpack.

"Stop," Steve ordered. "I know there's a Denny's here. I can smell it. Besides, we went to Gretzky's last time." He stopped in the middle of the sidewalk, visibly moving his head from left to right and sniffing the air. He pointed behind them. "Turn around. Follow me." He led the way at a somewhat slower pace as Jacob shook his head, smiled, and followed. "I don't know what your hurry is," Steve complained. "We should really stay another night. We got here too late to do any real partying."

"Things to do, people to see, Stevie. Someday when we're idle billionaires, we'll spend a year here so we can see every color G-string they have." Jacob's frustration with Steve's need to carouse was starting to show.

"Promises, promises! Doesn't your head hurt at all?" Steve had been rustled out of bed at 7 a.m. when Jacob, already showered and dressed, turned all the lights on in their hotel room. Steve showered while Jacob got a head start on coffee, cleaned his lenses, and checked his email. Jacob wasn't the only one frustrated this morning.

"Okay," said Jacob, "but let me stop in here and get a mocha. That Denny's coffee reminds me of a police station." They stopped in at a coffee shop and got in line. It was a large location, with two fully equipped barista stations, three registers, and seating for about fifty. Jacob's mind was already racing with ideas. The meeting with the Springfield boys was still fresh in his mind, and their story, if they could prove it, would be unique. It would be a significant piece in the puzzle he and Andreas had been working on for the last few years. But it still wouldn't be enough. There was still something missing. The *why*.

And, the *why* was what everyone was looking for.

A face he thought he recognized glanced into the front window of the coffee shop as the body attached to it walked briskly past.

He knew he had seen that face.

Time seemed to have frozen. Suddenly, Jacob dashed into the street, yelling at Steve to get him a mocha. He turned right and scanned both sides of the street for two blocks ahead. A second passed. He spotted her, already half a block ahead, almost at the corner. She glanced back and seemed to notice he was staring at her. She was a shapely woman in her mid-thirties and stood about five-foot-five inches tall. Her hair was very dark, and she had full lips. Her eyes looked Asian, possibly due to the makeup she was wearing. Where had he seen her? Somehow he knew this was important. He needed to stay in contact with her, but she might have seen him. The light was still red, and a solid stream of traffic blocked the street in front of her.

Now she was nervous, he could tell. Years of chasing camera-shy politicos and the power brokers behind them had honed his observation skills until he was like an Australian bush hunter stalking a big game animal. The woman kept adjusting the shoulder strap on her laptop bag, shifting from foot to foot and looking from left to right even though she knew traffic was solid for miles each way.

Jacob was slowly moving toward her, trying not to let her notice him. He wore a blue rainproof jacket and aviator sunglasses pushed up on his head. The seasoned photographer had unconsciously swung his backpack around on one shoulder and drawn his Nikon like an Old-West marshal drawing his six-gun. He held the body in his right hand, his left supporting the zoom lens, ready for the moment she would turn toward him. If he could make it to the corner before she disappeared in the traffic, he might be able to get a side-shot.

He didn't have to. The light turned green, and the woman half-turned to look back before quickly crossing the street, almost running. Jacob snapped nine exposures in two seconds. He would have a profile and a near straight-on shot.

He had no idea who she was.

Steve ate a bite of fried egg, a bite of sausage, a bite of bacon, then another bite of sausage, and another bite of egg. He looked like he was starting to feel much better. Sitting across from him, Jacob shoved a donut into his face as he stared at the series of nine high-resolution photos on his laptop. One after another, he flipped through them, back and forth, almost in rhythm with Steve's protein assembly line. He took a long drink from a tall paper cup bearing the logo of the coffee shop. It pictured a smiling girl with long, wavy hair. Around the border of the logo were the words "Norwich Coffee Shop."

"Ring any bells?" Steve asked as Jacob stared at the image of the woman on the street. He had only been slightly surprised when his buddy disappeared from the coffee line and ran from the shop, screaming, "Mocha!" It wasn't the first time his friend had chased down a photo. Jacob had explained to him long ago that freelancers—successful freelancers, that is—have to be ready in seconds when something happens or the right person comes into view. Those are the times when they get paid off for lugging around that backpack everywhere. But this was just a hunch. Jacob didn't even know who she was.

"Nothing," Jacob muttered, shutting the lid of his laptop. "I gotta get back home." His phone rang. It was a text message from Andreas. He must be in a library. He rarely used text, one of those generational things. He had verified some of the Logan info.

CHAPTER SEVEN

MONEY

Glowing blue-grey, the walls of his Manhattan apartment greeted Jacob as he awoke and sat up in bed. He stared at his window and silently cursed himself for leaving the curtains open the night before. A mental struggle commenced calculating the effort required to stand, walk to the window, close the curtains, and return to bed. He imagined how dark the room would be. Dark grey.

Jacob had returned late the night before. He had already put in a regular evening's work at WXNY-TV as a camera operator when a squall had rapidly developed close offshore. So, he had stayed for breaking weather reports into the early morning hours. Storms were always welcome because they meant overtime. His whole Boston and Toronto trip had been financed by extra shifts he took during Hurricane Irene. Media work allowed Jacob to be flexible so he could work on his missing passenger investigation.

Not that he could get time off anytime he needed it. Sometimes he just had to quit and hope for another position later. Freelance work helped him fill in those gaps. He had been putting in as much work as possible since returning from the convention because he needed to do some more traveling.

Before he could decide whether to close the curtains, get up, or try to sleep with them open, his cell phone rang. Rolling out of bed, he walked to the kitchen counter and picked up the phone. It was Andreas.

"It's no use. I need money," Jacob said, anticipating Andreas' question.

"Well, good morning to you too," Andreas spat sarcastically. "Sounds like you need a hurricane."

"I wouldn't wish another twenty billion dollars damage just so I could make a few hundred," Jacob said. "I have to go see those guys up in Mass, and I really need to make a Cleveland trip too."

"I know. Sometimes a face-to-face encounter is the only way. Plus, you need to get video interviews, I guess. Right?" Andreas sounded pretty upbeat.

"You know," said Jacob, "if this is going to turn out to be a full-length film, we could get the old gang involved. They sure sounded interested up in Boston. And they might have some freakin' cash!"

Andreas laughed a little. "Well, I was always open to the idea. I knew that was what you did when we started all this. Listen, I've been working on a theory based on the passenger list anomalies."

"Shoot," said Jacob. At that point, he thought, anything new was good.

"We know two hijackers were missing from American Flight 11," said Andreas. "The FBI said they were there, but the numbers don't add up. American Airlines reports ninety-two passengers and crew. The FBI says five hijackers were on the flight. That makes eighty-seven passengers and crew, but victim families verify eighty-nine. That means only three hijackers."

"This we already knew," Jacob shot back. "We assume the victims' families are correct." He sat down on the edge of his bed. "You were going to put together an exhibit, a full list with Internet references from tribute websites—"

"And photos too," Andreas added. "I just sent you a PDF. I've got the whole thing organized now."

"Sorry, please continue."

"AND from the Moussaoui trial evidence, we have the names of those five guys," Andreas went on. "If we can get the seat numbers of the two victims not accounted for in the official passenger list, we can determine which hijackers were not on the plane. Presumably, they survived and could still be alive somewhere or not. Either way, whatever their story is—it's probably a huge part of this whole mystery."

Jacob got up, walked to the kitchen area, turned on the coffee pot, and searched the cabinets for some coffee. "Andreas, I assume you have a job for me."

"Sure," said Andreas, audibly smiling. "Wanna go to Saudi Arabia and interview the hijackers?"

"You have GOT to give up the crack pipe, man," Jake replied. "You've hit bottom!"

"Well, in our business, you have to believe in the impossible," Andreas said, returning to reality. He knew that finding the mysterious men would be a tall order *if* they existed and were still alive. "I think the bay state boys will have to help us here. If the flights were split up, did two of the hijackers stay on the original Flight 11? If so, maybe the other three are the ones that are still alive. We need to nail this down." Andreas was matter-of-fact as if Jacob didn't already know the Massachusetts info was necessary, even critical.

"Which brings me back to my first point? Dinero? Shekels?" Jacob finally had the coffee going and poured a splash of milk into a large red coffee cup with the *Coast to Coast AM* logo on it.

"Don't look at me," said Andreas. "You're the one with the day job."

"Thanks, AB. You've been a big help," Jacob said, echoing his partner's earlier sarcasm.

"Good luck," said the older man. They hung up, and Jacob poured his first cup of coffee, looking determined to fund the next stage of his project. He looked at the clock on his microwave. *Way* too early to call Josh. In fact, it had been way too early to call Jacob. What was that old man thinking?

Jacob was wearing a long-sleeve t-shirt and boxers, his year-round sleepwear. He took a sip of the piping hot coffee, then set down the coffee and pulled on his sweatpants. There was not much to do now. He didn't have to be at work until mid-afternoon. No way to make any money until then. He toasted a bagel and went to his desk.

The most recent email was from Andreas and included an attachment. The text said, "Jake – here's a presentation I put together with all of the passenger discrepancy theories and supporting documents organized and linked. Should be suitable for presentation to John and Pete, Josh and Ty, or whoever else gets involved." He opened the attachment and paged through it. The first page displayed a standard passenger diagram of an American Airlines 737, with passenger names to each side of the fuselage at each row and the crew names at the top and bottom of the page. The next page had all the numerical information simplified and summarized. Then came the list of passengers, crew, and hijackers, each with a passport-sized photo and a short bio, including an Internet tribute link if available, plus victim family contact info.

Paying more attention to his breakfast than the screen, Jacob paged through the presentation. Suddenly, something registered in his brain, almost subconsciously, that made him stop, put down the bagel, scoot his chair forward, and lean toward the screen. He went back a page in the document, looking closer at each entry in the list. Near the top, with the other crew members, was the paragraph about Julie Foley, Flight Attendant. He focused on the photo, then glanced away as if trying to remember something. Then his eyes lit up, and he looked back down and pulled up the pictures from the Toronto trip. His photos were well organized, but it took him a moment to get past some more recent images to the set taken the weekend before.

Finally, he pulled up the files representing all nine bracketed shots of the woman on the street. He flipped back to the passport photo and zoomed in on it to compare the two side by side. It was a match! The more recent photograph was obviously of someone a few years older, and her hair was longer, but the features were just the same. He had just found a 9/11 casualty, alive and well. And he had proof! A smile crept over his face, one of satisfaction over a job well done. Then he became very serious. He closed the laptop lid and walked toward the window with his coffee, thinking. This would have to be handled just right.

"I have to lock it down," Jacob said to himself. Making an about-face, he rushed back to the desk and opened the laptop again. He copied the new pictures of Julie to an SD flash memory card, then ran a shredding program to eradicate them from his hard drive. He removed the card from its slot, put it in a hide-a-key box, then went to the fuse box behind the front door. He attached the magnetic hide-a-key to the inside of the fuse box door. He remembered there was a backup copy on his camera, so he grabbed it off a shelf near the desk and erased the files from the backup memory chip. He slumped in the chair behind his desk, breathing a sigh. He tried to think of what he needed to do next. The clock said 8:46. He couldn't delay any longer. He needed cash to take a leave of absence and go get this story. He needed to contact Josh and Ty. He crossed the room for his cell phone, then started writing a text message:

HENRY THOMAS AIKEN 10 A.M. TODAY

He sent the message to Josh and Ty. Josh responded immediately with "WILCO." Jacob started making a list of what he needed to do and steps to take to locate Julie. The most challenging thing he had to do was to get word to Andreas. They had no pre-arranged code or meeting place, and Andreas lived in Virginia, too far away. Jacob didn't have time to go, but maybe Ty or Josh could. Andreas's perspective on this would be critical.

Of course, there was no guarantee that Julie would cooperate. There could be any number of explanations for why she was still alive, but whatever the case, it was clear she did not want the general public to know she was alive. No one she had known before September 11, 2001, knew. Her name was on a plaque at the North Pool of the memorial at Ground Zero. It was read on TV every year. Her family had set up a foundation in her name devoted to protecting animals and furthering education, causes important to her. All of this was in the material Jacob had received that morning.

He wrote on his list that he needed to study Julie's life, everything he could find: her likes and dislikes, the kind of people she was attracted to as friends and lovers. This was another reason Jacob needed to contact his partner in Virginia.

Andreas would know where to find information that you couldn't find by typing her name in a search engine. Only by knowing her could he find her. And only by knowing her could he convince her to talk once he did find her.

CHAPTER EIGHT

HENRY THOMAS AIKEN

Josh stared down at the name Henry Thomas Aiken engraved at the South Pool of the 9/11 Memorial. The memorial included two fountain pools representing the former footprints of the World Trade Center's twin towers, with the water flowing down four fifty-foot walls to the pools. There was also a museum building at the site. The memorial was only completed in 2011 and opened at the annual remembrance service for the victims' families. The North Pool displayed the names of the passengers of Flight 11, the World Trade Center North Tower victims, and the 1993 World Trade Center bombing victims. The names of victims from the other three 9/11 flights, and those on the ground at the World Trade Center South Tower and the Pentagon, including first responders of which Mr. Aiken was one, were displayed at the South Pool. There was still some green on the many trees in the park surrounding the pools and the museum. The color was prominent on this sunny but very cool morning in Lower Manhattan.

Since it opened to the public, this site had been the pre-arranged meeting place for Josh and his friends. If they got separated in a protest or some other event, they met up at the South Pool. Or one of them would text a victim's name along with a meeting time. First responders were preferred because their stories were less controversial.

Josh was anxious and had not been sleeping very much. Life had been so exciting and rewarding the last few years. He didn't want to fall into a rut. Josh wanted to be on the cutting edge, gathering and disseminating information. It was getting more difficult as the years passed. The public information had already been reviewed or was so dense that it took a huge budget to sift through it. Information that remained hidden was buried deeper or forgotten or dying with the few individuals who possessed that knowledge. Vague myths such as your average paranoiac spouted while asking for your loose change was useless and more and more voluminous every day. And page after page of internet conspiracy garbage diluted the hard-hitting research on which he prided himself. So when he had been awakened by Jacob's text that morning, it didn't matter that he had only been asleep for two hours. He had immediately responded and started getting ready for anything.

A voracious reader since elementary school, Josh had gone through a time in junior high school when he read nothing but spy books. He had devoured all of Ian Fleming's works in a couple of months, followed by Robert Ludlum's Jason Bourne novels and the works of Ken Follett. By his second year in high school, Josh had read *The Art of War* and many non-fiction books on espionage and undercover private and police investigation, primarily surveillance. In the open, he could spot sloppy operatives from a block away, just by the way they moved their heads or where they stood in relation to points of egress and crowd movements. So it was not by mistake that Josh chose this meeting place. Even when someone else suggested a meeting, he wanted to have an advantage.

Josh turned around to face away from the pool and leaned his five-foot, eleven-inch frame against the panel where Aiken's name was engraved. A strong wind fluttered the navy North Face jacket he wore over a New York Mets fleece pullover and faded jeans. There were good reasons why these precautions were necessary. Text messages were recorded at cell towers, could be monitored by intelligence agencies, and were definitely monitored in the case of certain targeted individuals. At any one time, this list could include almost anyone. The law had not required warrants since shortly after 9/11, a presidential fiat that had not been successfully challenged in the courts and had been continued under the current administration.

But as far as Josh was concerned, the legality of the monitoring didn't matter. It would only matter if the government wanted to prosecute him with it. His concern was not that he might be prosecuted but that the wrong people might get important information, possibly damning to the powers that rule, before *everyone* got the information. And that those people might prevent the information from getting out. Since the day he started this work, all that mattered was getting the truth to as many people as possible.

Jacob turned the corner of the South Pool to Josh's right. He must have circled around, Josh thought, his anticipation escalating at the precautions Jacob was taking. Following protocol, Jacob walked up and whispered in his ear.

"Picasso." They turned and walked away in separate directions.

About half an hour later, Josh walked into Picasso's Pizza several blocks away. It was surprisingly roomy inside. There were windows across the front. The serving counter and cashier were across the back with the kitchen behind it. Under the serving counter were glassed-in shelves where pre-made pizzas were kept warm. There was a short hallway on either side of the serving counter, leading to restrooms, storage closets, and the kitchen. Josh made his way to a booth near one of the hallways at the back of the seating area. Jacob was already there, waiting for him. Josh slid in across from him.

"If you just wanted a slice, we could have avoided Ground Zero." Josh tried to use humor with his partners to downplay the seriousness of the work they did together and the ominous and sometimes morbid subject matter they dealt with. He smiled, but Jacob didn't. Jacob still looked nervous but confident as well. His face betrayed the fact that he was holding something that was a burden to hold. Something hot. Josh knew this feeling. He hadn't recognized it until after *Freefall* came out on YouTube and got over a million hits the first month. Suddenly he wasn't holding on to secrets anymore, and that burden had been lifted—until today.

Josh looked his friend in the eyes. "Okay. What is it?"

Jacob took out his phone and turned the screen so they both could see it, looking around to make sure they weren't being watched. On the screen was the old portrait from Andreas's presentation. "Julie Foley. Flight Attendant on one of the Logan flights. AA 11. Taken in 2001." He pressed a button that displayed the next photo. "And I took this one last week." He slowly flipped back and forth between the two to facilitate the comparison. Josh nodded and visibly accepted the new burden.

"What do you need?" Josh asked.

"I spoke to Andreas early this morning—not about this." Josh's eyes had widened, then his head dropped in instant relief. "You're in if you want in."

"We want in," Josh said, cutting in.

"I figured you would," Jacob said. "Anyway, I need a couple thousand. Enough for the other half of my rent, plus enough to spend a week in..." He was almost afraid to say it out loud. "...Toronto."

"And you'll need more if that isn't enough time," Josh added.

"Yeah. Where's Ty?" Ty had never answered the original text message.

"Girlfriend's," said Josh. "I called him about the text. Why?"

"I need to get word to Andreas and get him up there with me if he'll come."

"Don't worry; we'll take care of it." Josh's tone was positive and reassuring. "You know, this probably isn't the time to mention it, but I think there's a distributor that will let us keep editorial control. And with what you have now, trust me, no matter what else you get, that's enough. We're going to bust this thing wide open, and it'll be exclusive."

"Thanks, man. Hey, why don't we get a slice?" Jacob said, sliding out.

"Sure. Get me one too." Josh handed Jacob some cash as he speed-dialed his cell. "Tyler? Pack for a few days camping and meet me at the post office." As the sun reached its full height, the restaurant began to fill with tourists and workers.

As he walked up with two plates holding slices of pizza in one hand and two sodas in the other, Jacob said, "We need to set a code. If she'll talk, I'll want lights and a nice room." He had obviously been a waiter at some point in his diverse employment history. Setting everything down, he was visibly more relaxed, having shared his burden with someone else. "You know how these things go. A preliminary interview might be the only interview."

"How about something new that we both want to read?" Josh suggested. "Then it won't be a total waste of money." They were talking about an Ottendorf cipher, also known as a book code. Encrypted messages would contain some variation of numbers that referred to pages, lines, words, or characters in a book that both sender and receiver knew and could access.

"Sure," Jacob answered. "We'll hit a bookstore. I hope you didn't have anything planned today."

"Other than this? Not anymore." Josh took a drink of his soda. "I've already told Ty to meet me, though, so we shouldn't delay too long. By the way, is your stuff backed up?" They both were professionals and knew what that meant. If anything happened to them, their important work could only continue if the data was preserved.

"I'll update the box on my way out," Jacob replied. "I'm ready to go if you are." They hurriedly finished their slices and walked out to hail a cab.

Ty sat down on the steps of the Farley Building, Midtown's enormous post office, staring at 8th Avenue and Penn Station across the street. He had just gone inside to use the restroom after sitting for an hour. Sitting next to him was a large backpack that wasn't completely full. It was at times like this that he thought about the homeless. They mostly kept out of sight, especially during the day. But in New York, and to a lesser extent Boston and DC, you naturally spend a lot more time outdoors, walking around, or on buses and trains—mixing with other people. In places that aren't so densely populated, people spend more time in cars. And many people that live on the street are only there because they lost their jobs. That can happen to anyone. Ty's own economic situation was sometimes hand-to-mouth and never secure, but he still didn't know jack about being homeless. Although, he thought, smiling to himself, if Josh didn't show up soon, he might think this over in more depth.

A hand appeared in front of Ty's face, a rental car key dangling from it. "Bout time," he said. "It's almost sunset. Coffins are opening up all over town."

Josh smirked.

"I don't know this guy, and he doesn't know me," said Ty. Josh had given him a rough sketch of his mission in an email earlier. Ty was to drive to Lexington, VA, and meet Andreas face-to-face without scaring the crap out of him. Then he had to explain what was going on, that Jacob needed him, the need for secrecy, etc. After that, all he had to do was help the old guy in whatever way he could. In Ty's opinion, he had about a ninety percent chance of succeeding.

"Okay, Jake is going to give him a call in response to their conversation yesterday morning, which was not directly related. At least, it didn't involve the new information." Josh looked around to make sure no one was too interested in their conversation. Ty grabbed the keys, and Josh put his hands in his pockets against a deepening cold. He could see his breath as he spoke. "He's just going to say that we've become their partners in the film part of the project and will be assisting, financially and otherwise. Andreas already knows a little about us, but Jake is going to send him bios and recent pix anyway. So hopefully, when you show up, he'll recognize you."

"I'm thinking about calling him," Ty said. "You know, just say I'm passing through; suggest we grab a cup of coffee." Ty was getting charged about getting back to work again. This was what they all loved to do. There had been a long stretch of hosting booths like the one at *TruthCon*, appearing on radio shows, marketing the film, and looking for new ideas that never seemed to materialize. All the while, he knew Jake was working, albeit working very slowly. He was now looking forward to the chase once again.

"Sounds warm and tasty," Josh said with no emotion. Then, perking up, he continued, "I've got an idea. Why don't you get on the road, and I'll go get myself a cup of coffee!"

"Don't want me to drop you off?" Ty joked.

"Uh, you just did," said Josh. "The train station's across the street." He pointed as he spoke, then quickly returned his hand to his coat pocket. "By the way, the car's in the parking garage, level three. It's a silver Explorer. And here,"—he reached inside his coat and produced a new paperback book, still in the bag from the store—"it's the new primer. Jake has one too."

"Listen," said Josh, "if you guys get any video at all—and you will—get it back to me ASAP through secure channels. I'll need to start cutting right away. Meantime, I'm going to talk to Webloid again about funding." Josh would be the "home office" for this project, putting together the initial edit, securing post-production resources, securing funding, and doing whatever the production team needed while they were in the field. It was a role he'd played before, and he was good at it. Everyone seemed to be falling into their old roles.

Ty and Josh walked across the street. Ty slapped Josh on the back as he walked in the direction of the garage. "See ya."

"Yeah, be safe," said Josh, walking toward the light and warmth of Penn Station, visualizing a steaming cup of coffee and a smooth ride home.

CHAPTER NINE

NORTH

Ripping open the bulging envelope, Jacob dumped its contents out on the car seat next to him. Among them were a digital tape, a sealed number ten envelope containing his will and a list of all his financial assets (such as they were), and several recordable CDs with labels scribbled on them in black and red Sharpie. One said, "2002 Financial." He sifted through the items. He wouldn't have time to screen all the data to make sure it was still needed. But he was able to take a couple of the CDs and the tape out.

He put the rest of the items into a new UPS flat-rate box, dropped in an additional USB memory stick containing the info he had received recently from Andreas, along with the latest photos of Julie and a brief description of the events surrounding the taking of the pictures. He closed the box, attached a pre-printed adhesive label, then got out of the car into the light rain, which had just recently begun to fall. He walked around the driver's side door, which he left open, pulled down the door on the UPS dropbox, and inserted the parcel.

Later, the maroon Hyundai's wipers rapidly pulsed across the rain-soaked windshield to reveal the monotonous pavement ahead. It was almost 1 a.m., and the car and its occupant were approaching I-90. With virtually no traffic, Jacob could occasionally glance through side windows at the thick foliage dressing the right-of-way. It was dark, like a curtain drawn around his activity, isolating it. There was no beauty to it. The Interstate was entirely split by a hundred yards of this thick woods, so even oncoming headlights were not visible from the northbound lanes. Jacob drifted into a melancholy recollection of his origins, as he tended to do when forced to make a long, lonely trip like this. He often wondered why he was doing this instead of working on computers or selling cars for a living, or even having a regular media career. Instead, he was jumping around, trying to exist in the mainstream world for money, while making the alternative media—where there was no money—his career.

The disaffected, those who have a persistent skepticism regarding the government as opposed to the more common general low regard for bureaucracy and political dishonesty, often trace their orientation to a harmless curiosity followed by Socratic investigations into one story after another. Inevitably, there arises a pattern of lies couched as marketing, public relations, or political rhetoric. People thus informed develop a natural prejudice toward official pronouncements. Jacob's experience was not of this kind. His views were formed from personal experience.

Jacob was only eight years old when his father started having trouble with his kidneys. A Marine tank officer, he had served in Gulf War I and planned on continuing his military career. He got sick in 1995 and received a medical discharge. More ailments followed in the years to come, and Jacob's mother started to have the same problems. Blood tests showed that both were suffering from depleted uranium (DU) poisoning. The illness was similar to radiation sickness, contracted from working close to munitions containing DU, such as the 120mm sabot rounds fired from the M1 Abrams tanks used by Marines in Iraq in the early 1990s. As a teenager, after his father's death from leukemia, Jacob was shocked to learn that DU poisoning could be sexually transmitted, which was how his mother contracted it. She died two years later, also of leukemia.

All of this might have jaded Jacob. But the thing that put him over the edge was the VA's rejection of his parents' claim for disability benefits. Even though his father's problems had begun when he was still on active duty, the government said they were not related to his service. Jacob admired his father and reflected the personal pride he displayed every time he put on his uniform. He knew the job was dangerous and that this made his father's service all the more significant. Jacob learned what sacrifice was as he watched his father go to war. When the government abandoned his family to die of war wounds, he learned a new lesson.

Now, he had no close family. He had girlfriends on and off but never stayed with one for long. Steve was his closest friend, though they had not been as close since Steve got married and moved to Boston. As much as he moved around in his day jobs, he knew many people in broadcasting, but none of them well.

"The Box," as he called it, was a post office box in Squirrel Island, Maine. It contained an envelope, or sometimes a cardboard box, which contained the information Jacob wanted someone trustworthy to have if anything happened to him.

If he needed to add or remove anything, he retrieved the package, made the changes, then mailed the box to himself. If he were in a hurry, as he was this time, he would have Steve drive up and get it. Josh and Ty also knew about The Box, as did Andreas.

There were several advantages to this method and some disadvantages. The information, most of it, was all available in Jacob's apartment somewhere. But Jacob figured that someone could show up any time and steal or destroy it. Similar things had happened to others in the alternative media. The information they worked with was so controversial it evoked fear in the hearts of the powerful, and they sometimes reacted violently. But The Box was not on the Internet, and it wasn't in his apartment. The address wasn't written anywhere, and it wasn't on a computer anywhere. The only clues were the two generic keys held by Jacob and Steve. And even if one of them were compromised, it would still take time to get to Squirrel Island. It was only accessible by ferry or very small aircraft, perhaps enough time for one of the good guys to get there first.

As the Hyundai hummed down the road at seventy-five miles per hour, another glowing green sign zoomed at the windshield like a bad 3-D movie. Temporarily at peace with the course of life that had put him on I-90 Westbound at one a.m., he decided to stop for the night. He chose a 70's-era motel at the next exit, checked in, drove up to the room door, stumbled through it with his duffle bag, and collapsed on the bed.

CHAPTER TEN

SOUTH

O ff to the east was blackness punctuated by pulsating red lights atop the Key Bridge. On this moonless night, the Chesapeake Bay was an unseen presence lurking below. Patches of fog obscured some city features to the west where streetlights were just glowing centers of urban nebulae drifting by at seventy miles an hour. Ahead lay only white lines, dark pavement, and the pale yellow glow of the mouth of the Fort McHenry Tunnel. The silver Explorer plunged in without slowing down. As he drove under Baltimore Harbor, Ty wondered why people built tunnels instead of bridges. It had to be a lot more expensive. It was not as pleasurable to drive in a tunnel. He hit the mute button on the radio as Metropolitan Country turned into static.

When he emerged, it seemed colder, perhaps an illusion as the warm yellow light of the tunnel gave way to the charcoal grey of night punctured by the occasional street light. This route didn't pass through the gentrified urban center of the Inner Harbor but efficiently traced a path through what most of Baltimore truly was—an old-school industrial center. Ahead was a brewery, all corrugated steel and copper piping. To the right was a steel mill which might have been operating two or three shifts in better times but was now dark and cold overnight. Near the water was the campus of Lockheed Martin Naval Electronics and Surveillance Systems.

Later, as Hank Williams Jr.'s "Keep the Change" played on his radio, Ty drove past a black mirror-surfaced building with no lights at all. It was just a big hole in the suburban landscape, surrounded by thousands of parking spaces. He knew it was the massive headquarters of the National Security Agency. A quarter of a mile down the Interstate was an exit sign that said: "NSA Employees Only." Even at this time of night, he knew there must be a lot of activity behind those walls. As Fort Meade faded in the rear-view mirror and Hank faded into a commercial for a local law firm, Ty wondered what they were up to.

CHAPTER ELEVEN

CHI MESSAGE

"I need a Chi message sent," said M3, poking his head in the door of C3's office. Almost immediately, he dreaded the incomprehensible response he was sure to get from such a statement.

"Huh? Oh. One of your systems broke down?" C3 smirked, leaning back in his executive chair behind a virtually barren desk with a shiny, dust-free glass top, obviously enjoying his coworker's discomfort.

It was 0300 (3 a.m.). The two men wore black suits, white shirts with French cuffs, and black ties. They were both thirty-something and white with dark hair. C3, the Communications Division's night-shift director, had a large, lean frame and looked like he might have played basketball in college. He tapped a gold pen on the black leather-wrapped arm of his chair, rocking back and forth, only slightly moving. His cufflink was a silver death's head.

M3 walked through and let the door close behind him. The door was clear glass with black electric shutters on the inside. The walls of the office were also clear glass with black electric shutters. The shutters were closed on three sides. The shutters were open on the door and the wall surrounding it, revealing to the occupants a grey, carpeted walkway running past the office door. The walkway had a guardrail because beyond it was an open space to the floor below. A farm of cubicles resided there, designed in a similar style of clear glass framed in black. Some walls were all black, some all glass, some black on the bottom, and glass on the top. The ubiquitous fluorescent overhead fixtures lighted the scene. About half of the cubicles were occupied as were about half of the offices above, although the occupants seemed to move around a lot. The workers had white shirts and black ties and wore black pants or skirts. They moved between cubicles and between their own desks and a central area, which had a set of specialized security equipment used to code, decode, view, and transmit classified information. Every cubicle had at least three computer monitors and a safe.

M3 flopped into the chair in front of C3's desk. "Nothing's broken. H has a target visiting a known installation site for the second time in a week." H was the division responsible for Human Intelligence, also known as HUMINT.

The smirk was long gone from C3's face. He sat up straight in his chair with his feet flat on the floor. "Well, if H already has a man on him...."

"H has a man in New York City covering several targets," M3 said, interrupting. "This was unexpected. H is dispatching someone now, and the guy has to stop somewhere for the night." The frustration continued. Why couldn't C3 just give him what he needed? Every time M3 needed to contact a client, he had to go through this guy and explain every detail of what had happened up to that point.

"You mean their man lost the target?" The smirk was on its way back to C3's face. Another of his vastly inferior coworkers was falling down on the job.

"It doesn't matter. I still need that Chi message," said M3.

"Are you sure? Maybe it's just a coincidence? You have to have systems in New York that never got recalled." C3 didn't get all this code that M used. Messages and assignments always had a Greek letter associated with them. It never seemed to sink into his brain. It took him a few minutes to realize that Chi meant that the person (M3 sometimes called them "systems") in question had to return to his or her ("its") place of origin, the site where M's people had first made contact with him. Sometimes it was routine, but M3 wouldn't have taken the trouble to walk over to his office had this been routine. It would have been scheduled far in advance and communicated electronically through the usual channels.

"I'm sure, and it's important that we get it done quickly. It has to do with Big Wedding."

"Okay, your call. Do you have the protocol sheet? Wouldn't want to send your system running off the roof of a building by mistake," C3 smiled.

"Sure," said M3. "All that. Who's going to work it? I'll just give it to your man." M3 didn't want to slow things down and confuse C3 even further by leaving him the information needed to deliver the message properly. He would undoubtedly read it before passing it on to one of his minions for transmission.

"Uh, Faebaen, I guess. I'll tell her to expect it." As M3 hurriedly walked out, C3 leaned forward and picked up the receiver of his desk phone.

A young woman with long curly, dirty blonde hair pulled into a loose ponytail stood in front of what looked like a secure fax machine feeding in a sheet of paper. The badge clipped to the lapel of her black suit jacket read "Faebaen," and underneath it, "Communications." Written across the top of the sheet of paper she was feeding into the machine were the words "National Security Agency."

Six a.m. Syracuse, New York. Refreshed and ready for whatever battles lay ahead, Jacob emerged from his hotel room with his backpack on. After paying his bill and dropping off the key, he pocketed the receipt to send to Josh later. The Hyundai was right where Jacob left it and was a lot dirtier than it had been the previous evening when he picked it up in Manhattan. He put the backpack in the passenger seat, then took a moment to look around. Day was breaking, but there was a ceiling of clouds, and though he could see areas of orange and purple light, they were sparse. The Interstate hummed as it always did, with few breaks in the rushing air sound that was really tires on the pavement a mile away.

There was a light fog on the ground. The mist was elusive but everywhere. Anytime Jacob got close to it, it seemed to fade away and get thicker in the distance. It reminded him of the story he was after. Jacob took a last deep breath of the crisp November air before sealing himself in the little rental car for the next four hours. The challenge was ahead, but for now, everything seemed to be alright.

Across the street was a Giant Eagle gas station. Above the door was an eagle logo that looked like the one on the Great Seal of the United States. In the far-left parking spot was a black Chevy Caprice that was just as dirty as Jacob's car. The clean-cut man sitting at the wheel wore a light jacket over a casual-style shirt. His hand was on the steering wheel, and on it was a silver ring that also bore an eagle. The eagle held a key in its talons.

The man looked across the street through some light fog and watched Jacob climb into his vehicle. He started the car and took a sip of coffee from a paper cup. Putting the coffee back in its place in the console, the clean-cut man put the car in gear and entered the street. He was just close enough behind the maroon Hyundai that he could still see it in the light early morning traffic. As they moved onto I-90 and got up to speed, the fog seemed to thin a bit, the glow from beyond the clouds growing slightly brighter.

Jacob settled in for a long ride, pressing the buttons on the steering wheel to scan through radio stations. He was trying to find a talk station, anything to keep him engaged and not hypnotized by the white line stretching out for miles in front of him. He was pleased about the overcast weather as it was easier on his eyes as he drove. Something about the fog and the clouds created an atmospheric effect that made it seem like Niagara Falls, just a few hours' drive ahead. Inexorably, Jacob's mind soon returned to the initial task he would face when he reached the destination: finding Julie Foley. Unless she had noticed him, which didn't seem likely, she would probably still follow her regular routine. He could use that to his advantage since, unless Julie was a real intelligence agent or just paranoid, she probably did the same things every day, as most working people did. So she would be in the same places while he tried to find her. Hopefully, those places were near where he had spotted her, and that was where he would start.

CHAPTER TWELVE

LIAM

A slim man with dark, straight hair that hung over his ears walked into the lobby of a small high-rise apartment building. As he stopped to retrieve his mail at a wall of small boxes with locked doors, someone walked up behind him, greeting him with a mumble. It was the kind of greeting that allows one to recognize the person extending the greeting but not to hear anything or have time to say anything in response. By the time he turned his head, she was walking into the elevator, a young woman he knew from similar brief encounters in the recent past. She probably had a laptop bag over her shoulder, would go up to her apartment on some floor other than the one he lived on, and, like most people who lived there, go in and not emerge until morning.

He pulled out a pack of bills and advertisements. The mail was all addressed to Liam Smith. He stood in the elevator, waiting for the doors to close so he could execute the same routine as the girl ahead of him. He wore a two-tone, zipper-necked smock with dark brown at the shoulders, sleeves, and chest, light brown below that. On his left breast was embroidered the name Liam in light brown against the dark brown background. On the right was the logo of the Norwich Coffee Shop.

Liam held a stern look on his face as if he was doing something he was required to do but was not necessarily interested in. As the elevator came to the building's top floor, his look suddenly changed to one of innocent surprise. He leaned down and touched his ankle, then noticed the doors were opening, upon which he straightened up and walked forward into the hallway. He hurried down the hall and into his apartment, locking the door behind him.

The apartment was a tiny efficiency. Next to the front door was a skinny door that led to a closet. It wasn't large enough for its intended use, as Liam had shirts and other articles hung elsewhere in the room, from the curtain rod, from a nail in the wall, from the back of a chair. Next to the closet was the door to the bathroom. A small built-in desk separated the bathroom from the kitchen area. On the other side of the room were a single bed and an overstuffed chair facing a small television.

He dropped the packet of mail on the built-in desk, then went to the overstuffed chair and sat. Bending over to his ankle again, he raised his pant leg, revealing a device in a leather holster strapped to his leg, secured by Velcro. A light was blinking on the device, indicating that it contained a new, unread message. He drew it, revealing a two-way text pager with a two-inch screen that glowed blue. He looked closely at the message. It consisted only of a three-digit number.

He replied to the message with only a zero and deleted it. He then quickly started getting undressed. He put on a pair of jeans that were lying on his bed. Then, he chose an orange t-shirt from a stack of folded clothes on a wire shelf on the wall. All of his shirts were short-sleeved, which was odd for Toronto, but he always wore a jacket. He put on the dark-blue North Face jacket, obviously well-worn and frayed in some places but functional, as he closed the zipper and walked out the front door.

Liam stepped off the back of a streetcar bearing the crown-shaped logo of the Toronto Transit Commission. It was about three P.M., and the sun was shining on the busy downtown street. A short walk from the streetcar stop, he walked into FedEx Kinko's to the sound of electronic bells triggered by the door opening. A few people typed at computer stations along the front window of the shop. Large printers loomed at the back, behind a counter. To the left of the counter was a matrix of square boxes open in front and back, marked by letters of the alphabet. A middle-aged man dressed in a starched button-down shirt with an embroidered logo stepped up to a cash register as Liam approached.

"Can I help you?" he asked. Liam had been here only a few times in the previous year but had always assumed the man in front of him was the local franchise owner.

"Do you have a fax for Liam Smith?" Liam glanced at the matrix of boxes as he spoke, noticing a sealed number ten envelope along with some rolled-up sheets in the box marked "S." The middle-aged man looked through all of this, selecting the sealed envelope and replacing the rest of the material. Returning to the cash register, he moved the mouse to choose an item on his screen and clicked it.

"One sealed fax," said the man at the counter. "A flat rate of four ninety-nine plus tax is five seventy-four." Liam paid the man and then opened the envelope. There was a cover page with a Kinko's logo. The second page was blank except for a large square made up of apparently randomly placed smaller black and white squares. Having confirmed that the pages were there, he folded them up again and put them in his inside jacket pocket.

Glancing around the store, Liam considered the copier near an island in the middle of the store that offered fax cover sheets and other forms. Traffic in the store was relatively light. But he thought better of it and set out toward the street again, following a predetermined plan.

As the light was about to change against him, Liam ran through the crosswalk to the opposite corner. He scanned a schedule placard at a transit stop near the intersection, not finding a suitable entry, and continued down the sidewalk. He turned again, walked a block, and turned again. A few minutes later, he was at another Kinko's several blocks away. Inside, the store looked almost exactly like the other one. He entered and went straight toward the island in the middle as a young woman behind the cash register watched him for a second, then gazed out the front windows. Soon a customer walked toward her from the computers across the room, and she began checking him out.

Liam withdrew his wallet and removed from it a tiny micro-SD memory card. From his pocket, he produced an adapter that accepted the device. Together they were the size of a standard SD card. He inserted the combination into a slot on the copier. He pulled out the fax pages from his coat pocket and placed the page with the matrix image on the copier surface face-down. He selected the scan option and saved the image to the microSD card. He grabbed the card and the fax page from the copier and walked to the cashier.

"Can you shred this?" he said, handing her both pages of the fax. She took them to a shredder, and he watched her destroy the pages. He paid her for the use of the copier, then dropped the envelope into a trash bin on the way out the door.

Back in his apartment, Liam opened the closet door next to the front door. Inside was a small safe. He entered the combination, opened the door, and withdrew a small laptop computer. He turned it on and left it on his bed to boot up. While waiting, he went to his refrigerator, pulled out a Dr. Pepper, opened it, and took a drink. His face displayed that same look of profound boredom. He stared at the computer screen across the room with reluctant attentiveness. It seemed to be running additional start-up routines, checking various aspects of security. One said, "… scanning for unauthorized binaries…" Another, "…closing all network nodes…" And still another, "…nullifying all RF radiation wavelengths…"

Each process had sub-processes that ran and completed giving notifications on the screen.

After about twenty minutes, Liam had finished his Dr. Pepper, and his laptop had finished booting. He took it to the small built-in desk next to the kitchen area and plugged in a power cable that was already plugged into the wall socket there. Liam pulled the micro-SD card from his wallet and inserted it in a slot on the front of the laptop, which did not require the adapter he had used back in the copy shop. He started a program to interpret the encrypted data on the card.

None of the programs and graphics on this computer was a standard consumer program. Absolutely everything looked custom-designed. But after the decryption had run, a plain-text message appeared, accompanied by a picture of Julie Foley. In the middle of one page, in large letters, were the words CHARLIE CHAN. Liam studied the pages for a few minutes, then clicked on a shred program that started erasing the micro-SD card and any residual information stored on the computer. This process took a few minutes, executing multiple writes over the areas of storage that had contained the information he had just read. When it was done, the computer automatically shut down, and the screen went to black.

CHAPTER THIRTEEN

INTERCEPT

Jacob sat on a bench at a bus stop about half a block from the corner where he had first encountered Julie. It was high noon, and many people were walking around shopping, going to and from lunch, or just getting some air during their noon break from work. In contrast to the weather when he started his day, it was quite sunny with only a few clouds overhead.

He knew he was just playing the odds that she worked in the area. In actuality, he could be sitting there for the next year and never see her. But he had to start somewhere. It also got him out of the coffee shop, which would be busy during lunchtime. He had taken up a sort of residence there late that morning. And he hoped that she would pass by the following day at about the same time as before.

Jacob was wearing a light jacket over a navy University of Toronto t-shirt and jeans. He was trying to blend in but didn't feel like he was doing a very good job. Most of these people were wearing suits, or at least dress pants and button-down shirts. He got the feeling that this was the financial district.

Inside the Norwich Coffee Shop, Liam was staring out the front window while talking to the day shift manager and simultaneously filling the noontime crowd's coffee orders.

"Just this week, I need all the hours I can get." He needed to be in this area and unnoticed. The best way was to be working, so there would be no questions about *why* he was hanging about in the area for so long. Julie came by the shop on a semi-regular basis. Liam had seen her before and was confident that he was placed at Norwich for that reason. So he did not expect to have to go searching for her to complete his assignment. However, he did need to be at the shop as much as possible.

Except for the manager, all employees were part-time. More employees gave the management more flexibility and made the job attractive to potential employees while providing a fraction of the benefits available to full-time employees. Bob, the manager, was used to hearing pleas for more hours, especially from people like Liam, whom he knew had no other means of support. However, it had been a while since Liam had asked for hours. He was a good worker. Although he didn't have the level of enthusiasm in dealing with customers that Bob liked, Liam was always on time and was flexible enough to take hours when no one wanted them or take a few days off when business was slow.

"Schedule's made out through Wednesday. I'll do what I can for you after that. I think Wendy is taking a vacation. If so, you can have the bulk of her hours."

"Thanks." Liam was still staring out the window, still cranking out latte after cappuccino after café au lait, with the occasional Americano thrown in.

Andreas opened the front door. A grey cat made its way inside, deftly avoiding his leather hiking boots. "Hello, Matty," he said to her, walking out to the edge of his quiet street to get the day's mail. Birds chirped away, happy, he thought, that his cat Mata Hari had returned to the confines of his house. He didn't bother to look at the mail, cradling it at his side and shoving his other hand in the pocket of his jeans in the crisp air. It was overcast with a chill, but he had to squint in the glare as he looked up to check the status of the leaves on his two-decades-old white oaks.

Down the street about half a block, parked in front of a house with a real estate agent's sign out front and overgrown grass in the yard, Ty sat in the front seat of his rented Ford Explorer, half-humming, half-singing along with "Leaning on the Everlasting Arms," playing softly on the vehicle's radio. On long trips, he would listen to several styles of music to keep himself from getting bored or falling asleep. Gospel was just the latest of these. He was eating sunflower seeds from a bag on the seat next to him, occasionally looking through a set of binoculars toward the large mailbox with "Becker" in Old English lettering painted on the side. He had placed his message after the postman had passed through and watched to make sure it wasn't tampered with until retrieved. As Andreas closed his front door, Ty started the Explorer and drove away in search of a cheeseburger.

Having fed Mata Hari and put a pan of vegetable soup on the stove to heat up, Andreas now stood at his kitchen trash can, dropping in various pieces of junk mail as he flipped through the envelopes. About halfway through, he came across an envelope with no address and no stamp. On the front was written in ball-point pen "Open Now!" Andreas went immediately to the front window of his house and looked outside for any unfamiliar people or vehicles. Then he heard the soup boiling over and sizzling on the stove and rushed back to the kitchen to move the pan from the burner and turn it off.

He put the envelope and the rest of the mail on the table at the center of his small, but not cramped, kitchen. He poured the soup into a bowl he had already set on a plate with some crackers and put it all at his place at the end of the table. He was in no big hurry, as he didn't think whoever had left that envelope knew when he was going to collect it. He opened the refrigerator and took out a pitcher of tea, pouring it over a glass of ice. Sitting down, he took a drink of tea and a sip of the piping hot soup before leaning back a bit and opening the envelope.

The message was short and to the point. "I'm Jacob's friend Ty. Meet me at the Station Café at 3 p.m." He stared at the words for a minute, taking them in, looked at the clock, then set the note down on the table and turned back to his soup, crumbling some crackers into the bowl. He knew Jacob was getting these guys involved in the film. But why the cloak and dagger stuff? Why not just call him up if they needed to meet? He wondered if he should have a gun at this meeting, then dismissed the thought. All he had was a shotgun anyway. Not that it would be unthinkable in this town to stride into a downtown café with a gun. It would just be a bit unusual and would attract attention and questions about hunting.

Perhaps he shouldn't go at all. Maybe it was too dangerous. He picked up Ty's message and set it down again. He had spoken with Jacob a couple of days earlier, and nothing had been said about Ty or anyone else coming this way. And if they wanted to film him, surely they would have called ahead to be sure he would be home and prepared him with a list of questions or topics or something. It was all bizarre. Still, the café was a public place. There would be plenty of witnesses. If this person wasn't Ty and wanted to harm him, they could have just broken down the door instead of leaving a note. Maybe they wanted to search his place. There were just too many possibilities.

Andreas wondered if he should try to call Jacob to confirm this. Of course, Ty might have been coming down without Jacob's knowledge. The note didn't say not to call. Andreas pondered the options as he finished his soup. Matty wanted out again. He looked through the kitchen window. The wind was picking up outside, and the sun was starting to peek through the cloud cover. After he let his cat out and put the lunch dishes in the kitchen sink, he went toward the back of the house to the little office to get his cell phone.

Jacob was thinking about leaving the street bench he had been parked upon for the last hour. He had not seen Julie or anything else worth shooting. As Jacob considered his next move, his cell phone vibrated in his jacket pocket. He looked at the screen. It was Andreas. They shouldn't be talking. Ty should have spoken to him by now. He pressed the call button. "A.B! Good to hear from you!"

"Uh, yeah, Jake. I just wanted to check something out with you. Ty—"

Jacob cut him off. "Ty! Right. I want you guys to meet *real soon!*" He hoped Andreas could figure out from his inflections that he didn't want to say much of anything over the phone.

"You do? OK." Andreas could tell something was amiss, but he still wasn't sure. "*Real* soon? So—"

"Yes, A.B.," urged Jacob. "Now, if not sooner. I'm glad you mentioned it. But unfortunately, I'm in the middle of something right now, so I need to get off the phone. We'll talk soon, OK?"

"Sure. Thanks."

Hopefully, Andreas had gotten the message from their short conversation. Whatever was going on, he had to make that meeting.

CHAPTER FOURTEEN

STATION CAFÉ

Despite being a lifelong New Yorker, Ty loved the South. It was cliché to say people were friendly down there, but it was a natural kind of friendliness and not naïve. He knew that New Yorkers and Bostonians were friendly too, but in a completely different sort of way. In The Bronx, for example, a guy could say, "Screw you!" out of the kindness of a full and welcoming heart. In Boston, a person could look you straight in the eye without looking at you at all. That stuff never happened down here. People were just straightforward, honest, and polite. At least, that was his experience thus far. Maybe *he* was the naïve one.

The Station Café was nothing special, to look at the décor or the menu. It was a greasy spoon with checkered tablecloths, wooden booths, a bottle of Tabasco on every table, and a few metal signs advertising oil companies that hadn't existed for almost a hundred years. In the middle of the dining room was an antique "visible" gas pump. It was the kind that allowed a customer or attendant to pump the correct amount of gas into a glass holding tank that sat on top of the pump. Then the gas was drained by force of gravity into the tank of the customer's vehicle. The idea was that the customer wouldn't get fooled because he could see the gas before it entered the car. Here, of course, it was just decoration, but Ty thought it was a nice touch. He saw Andreas coming in the door. He was a tall man, sixtyish, but with a full head of hair that was pale blonde turning to grey in a manner that made one think he may have had no grey hair at all. His neatly trimmed beard matched. He wore wire-rimmed glasses and a dark flannel shirt over jeans and hiking boots. Ty stood and waved, smiling.

Andreas looked left and right, then back at Ty and returned the smile. "Glad you recognized me," quipped Andreas. There wasn't another soul in the place. It was completely abandoned, save for a large woman sweeping up behind a serving counter with a cash register on it. He stretched out his hand, and Ty shook it.

"Well, just trying to be neighborly," said Ty. "'When in Rome,' you know." They sat down, and the woman came around and started over to their table. "I thought you might be a little nervous."

"What's going on, Ty?" Andreas began. "I called Jake, but he didn't want to say anything." He turned to the woman, who was flashing a familiar smile. Andreas smiled back at her. "Betty, you don't usually wait tables."

"Well, we're kinda slow now," said Betty.

"I'll have some coffee." He and Betty looked over at Ty.

"Same!"

Betty walked away, stopping at another table to brush some crumbs off it. Ty turned back to Andreas with a knowing look. "It can seem like we're paranoid at times like this, but we've been burned enough times in the past."

"Burned how?" asked Andreas.

"It's usually just other people like us—filmmakers, journalists. The kind that makes a decent living from it and needs a constant stream of material. They can be unscrupulous at times."

"And the others?" Andreas asked in a tone that said he wasn't sure he wanted to know.

"Well, with this type of work, someone's always getting embarrassed," said Ty. "Often, someone with enough pull to put somebody in jail or get an injunction." Ty could see the worried look on Andreas' face, even at this suggestion of some of the milder possibilities. "But look, we're not worried. We're just cautious."

"Jake must have found something," said Andreas. The worry drained from his face, and excitement started to creep in. "Tell me."

Ty leaned over and looked left and right. Just then, Betty showed up with the coffee. "Here you go!" she said, setting a steaming urn on the table. "I'll leave the pot here since y'all are my *special* guests today." Then in a mock whisper, she said, "Actually, I'm just lazy, but don't tell anybody!"

"Thanks, Betty," said Andreas, returning her smile. He looked back at Ty. "Well?"

"You remember all that passenger stuff you put together?" Ty asked. Andreas nodded. "Jake saw one of those passengers when he was up in Canada."

Andreas's eyes widened. He looked very serious. "Wow," he said without inflection.

"He didn't even know until he got that stuff from you," Ty continued. "He had snapped a few shots of her on the street just on instinct. When he got that stuff from you, with the passenger pictures, he figured it out."

"Wow," Andreas repeated. "No wonder you guys are taking precautions."

"Jacob is already back in Toronto. He wants you to come up there. Our company is funding the whole thing, and I'm your chauffeur. What do you want to do?" Ty leaned back in his chair and took his coffee cup in both hands, then raised it toward Betty with a smile, acknowledging her coffee-making skill. Andreas was cogitating. "Take your time," Ty said, "let it sink in."

CHAPTER FIFTEEN

THE PASSENGER PROJECT

"We are going to have the usual interviews with various experts that any high-quality documentary contains." Josh sat back in a giant leather chair in an isolated nook of The Office, a trendy upscale speakeasy near Central Park. He was deep into his pitch for funding what he was tentatively calling *The Passenger Project* with Bill Sandusky, the head of Content Acquisition for Small Box Films. "But Bill," Josh continued, "the compelling part is going to be the testimony of a person with first-hand knowledge of the deception."

Sitting directly across from Josh, Sandusky stared attentively at the young filmmaker. Bill Sandusky had built Small Box Films from scratch by acquiring commercially ignored but compelling independent films and distributing them through Webloid, a company made famous by renting DVDs by mail and streaming them over the Internet. In addition to its millions of mail and streaming customers, Small Box had brokered deals in recent months to distribute its acquisitions to theatres as well. Theirs was a business environment where eighty percent of the money comes from a few blockbusters. Most distributors went with the sure thing, leaving a lot of good content available for Webloid's internet customer base. People who watch at least a couple of movies per week soon run out of blockbusters and hunger for new content.

Webloid had already offered Freefall Productions' other two films. The second one had racked up millions of viewings. Josh knew this type of film would do well with this audience, as did Sandusky. The real question was how much up-front funding Small Box would be willing to provide and what the split would be when the film was released. That's what Josh was really pitching for.

Though Sandusky needed to constantly acquire films and encourage independent filmmakers, his job was to be skeptical during negotiations. Most of the producers he dealt with had no idea how much money they really needed. They just figured more was better. By now, Josh was more savvy and professional, but he was still only one project removed from being an amateur. *Freefall 2* had gone $100,000 over budget, which was the main reason he was struggling now. Small films had to be lean, and the small film producer had to keep multiple projects going to stay afloat because some of them inevitably made no money at all.

"Josh," said Sandusky, "I'm not going to steal your idea or broadcast it to the world. I want you to succeed here with something special. But you're not telling me anything. How do I know you're not just rehashing what's already out there?"

"First of all," said Josh, "there isn't anything 'out there' to rehash. No one has made a film based on passenger discrepancies. Not even a ten-minute clip. But it's a compelling idea. Can't you admit that?"

"It could be compelling," agreed Sandusky, "and it could be just a mistake in the paperwork somewhere."

"Bill, this isn't just paperwork," said Josh, leaning forward. "The passengers and crew on those lists have families and friends. People who cared enough to hold funeral services for them; people who make pilgrimages to the memorials." Josh paused, then continued, "They left lives behind. So, what if some of them didn't die? Even one. Wouldn't that be compelling?"

Sandusky wanted to believe. He asked, "So you have some evidence of a survivor?"

"Bill, you know how cautious I am," Josh responded. "I already have Ty and Jake out on assignments, and we haven't discussed this on the phone *ever.* But I can tell you that we have enough right now to make this an important and viral film. With your help, we may be able to get something that will blow it up beyond even my wildest dreams."

"How much do you need up front?" asked Sandusky. "I need to discuss this with my board, of course." He was anxious to get on board, but he was really basing his decision on past successes. To date, Josh had not failed to come up with video gold.

"We're thinking of getting Tom Hanks to narrate." Josh knew that negotiation never really ended, but certainly not until the money was in his bank account. He almost chuckled to himself. Josh's statement was code to get the number into seven figures.

"He'll take a cut," the wily distributor shot back.

"Seven-fifty then. But we may need a second round in post." For low-budget documentaries using content from multiple sources and public archives, post-production could be as expensive as filming the original content and sometimes more costly.

Sandusky could have laughed, but he didn't. "Your last one made six-fifty—"

"So far," Josh cut in.

"So far, and may make a million someday. But you and Ty just started getting paid on it. And I certainly don't want to wait six months or a year before small paychecks start trickling in. Go leaner. You know, if you keep on in this business, someday you'll have a flop. You need to diversify and get some more projects going. Let's talk about that later. The final budget for *Freefall 2* was three hundred K. I think I can swing that. We'll talk again when you're in post, but I really think you should bring it in under *including* post."

"You're not gonna regret it!" Josh couldn't resist inserting some cheesy humor.

"OK, man, I gotta jet," Sandusky said. "You'll hear from us next week."

"Yeah, babe. Thanks." Josh said, shaking hands as Sandusky got up to leave. Josh was pleased. His funding mission was accomplished, or soon would be, and he had only spent a few thousand of his own money thus far. He knew it would be a few thousand more next week, though, so the timing was crucial. Of course, Bill was right about staying lean. But having extra money in the bank had no downside as far as Josh was concerned. It was just like getting paid earlier. He was confident that *Freefall 2* would break a million and that *The Passenger Project* would be even more successful. He was already thinking about running more than one project at a time, though, and they could use any leftover funds to start something new. If he could fund a film himself, the profit would be better on the back end. All these wheels were turning in Josh's head. He was starting to feel the pressure to make this film happen.

Josh sat in the makeshift office of Freefall Productions, which was actually the third bedroom of his and Ty's apartment. Thoughts raced through his mind, mainly of all the things that could go wrong with this project.

There was a small black desk in the middle of the room on which rested a laptop that was running a financial program. Also on the desk were various bills, receipts, and other paperwork. The room was narrow, but there was a ratty-looking blue loveseat on one wall. A tiny window looked out on the street and across to another high-rise. Around the sides of the room and on the floor were most of the items they had carried to *TruthCon*, including boxes of T-shirts and DVDs. Undoubtedly, more DVDs were stored elsewhere. Covering the dark wood-paneled walls were *Freefall* movie posters, maps, and blown-up photos of commercial wide-body jets, the steel framing of the World Trade Center buildings during their construction, and the 9/11 Pentagon damage as seen from a security camera. Several photographic light stands stood in a corner, folded up. Near the desk hung a calendar advertising a local camera shop.

When his phone rang, Josh didn't recognize the number. He touched a Bluetooth earpiece.

"Hello."

"Josh?" said a thick New England accent. "It's John Thompson. We met at *TruthCon*." Thompson waited for Josh to remember.

"Okay," Josh said, pulling up the memory of the booth and the few hundred people that visited it, then recalling their dinner in Boston. "Yeah, I remember. John from Springfield. The ghost flight. What's up?"

"We have something new," said Thompson. "I tried to call Jacob, but he didn't answer, and that was a couple of days ago." Josh could tell that Thompson might be slightly hard to get along with. Thompson reminded Josh of a lot of people from outside New York who were just too sensitive. Thompson was determined and stubborn. It was a rugged, All-American attitude, but one that would probably be a pain in Josh's backside, albeit perhaps a necessary one.

"Well, Jake's also found something new," Josh replied, "and he's out tracking it down, probably for a couple of weeks at least. Can I help you?" Josh tried not to show how excited he was and how eager to find out what new information John had. Recalling the dinner conversation in Boston, he remembered how riveted he was to the story John and Pete had told.

"Remember that security guard from Logan who died from a heart attack?" asked Thompson. "His death may not have been from natural causes."

"What makes you think so?" Josh wasn't sure if Thompson was grasping at straws. Sometimes an investigator, eager for more meat for his story, starts to speculate.

"It's probably impossible to prove," continued Thompson. "But there's something else: There may be video of him diverting those passengers." Josh was hooked. His mind raced. Caution.

"John, don't say another word. I'm coming up there; I'll contact you when I arrive," Josh said and ended the call. Okay, Josh thought, so much for a few thousand dollars next week. It's going to be this week. Sandusky had better come through now. He thought about sending the producer an email explaining the urgency but realized it wouldn't work. In the negotiating process, novice applicants, desperate for cash, sometimes used such tactics.

He stood up and looked around. He would need to take his "office" with him, everything he needed to play the producer role. He was also going back into the trenches to dig up some elusive video with his allies in Boston. His team needed another partner. An intern, he thought, that wouldn't need to be paid. He smiled at the thought as he located a backpack and started shoving in files, memory cards, a clip-on microphone wired to a radio transmitter. He would need clothes, another rental car.

Josh stopped packing, having reached over to close his laptop. He had to prioritize. Ty could stop on his way up North, and they all could figure out who would do what. He could think about it on the drive up. Josh sat down in front of the laptop and brought up his email program. Then he looked over, opened a drawer, and took out a new paperback book still wrapped in the plastic bag from the bookstore where he had bought it several days ago. As Josh removed the book from his bag, a receipt fell out on the floor. He picked it up and put it in one of the folders on his desk. Then he took out a ballpoint pen from the desk drawer, opened the book, and started encoding with the Ottendorf cipher. He used the pen to count letters in the book, then typed the code with one finger into a new email message.

CHAPTER SIXTEEN

THE RUB

Midnight. Josh sat in a very uncomfortable wooden chair in a hotel room with all the modern furnishings one would expect in 1989. Unfortunately, it was November 2011. Josh would typically ignore such things, but he had been away from fieldwork for a year or so. His accommodations at the Fairmont Copley Plaza had been much more to his liking. Outside, the temperature was already below freezing. Winter had now been underway in New England for almost a month. It had snowed once, and there was a chance of more that night. Across the street, floodlights lit statues of Dr. Seuss characters in a park. Beyond it, the spire of St. Michael's Cathedral towered in the shadows. Nights seemed deeper in the winter and deeper still the farther north one traveled.

Josh had driven the three hours from New York in a pickup truck he managed to borrow, wanting to save money and still very conscious of Bill's warnings earlier that evening about staying lean. There were no decent hotels in Springfield, so that temptation wasn't a problem. He kicked the heater for the second time.

"Cold enough for ya?" Pete Rodolpho sat in the only comfortable chair in the room with his feet up on a stuffed ottoman. John Thompson chuckled from his position seated on the bed. He wore a light cotton jacket. Pete had on a leather flight jacket that must have been made from several very large bovine animals.

"What about you guys?" Josh asked, irritated and shivering.

"Oh, it's still fall. I like the crispness in the air," Pete said in his thick New England accent, the 'r' in 'air' disappearing to somewhere, probably the same place where all the heat had gone. "When it gets really cold, I wear my snowsuit." Thompson continued to laugh along with Pete and started flipping through the contents of one of two accordion-style folders he had brought with him. Newspaper clippings, printed web pages, and printouts from microfilm readers soon covered the area around him. The other sat bound in its elastic band on the bed next to him. It contained the personal notes he had made over the last ten years.

Josh was starting to loosen up and laugh along with the two jolly men and wondered if they should all just go home and go to bed. Ty would probably be there in the morning, and Josh would have a clearer head, having slept on all the events of that day. But the guys had been willing to meet him, and they had families they could be spending the evening with. He recognized that this was more than a job for most people working on it. It was the role of Josh and people like him to bridge the gap and get the word out in a profitable way.

"OK guys, spill it," Josh said. "We're off the grid now. No phone lines or satellites to worry about. Tell me everything." Josh leaned forward in the chair and rubbed his hands together. He was still wearing his jacket.

"Did you sweep the room for bugs?" Pete asked. He was serious, even though he'd never swept for surveillance transmitters in his life.

"I think we're okay, as long as this isn't one of Whitey Bulger's old handouts," said Josh. Thompson and Pete glanced at each other and nodded. "Even I didn't know I was going to stay here until I got into town."

"To be honest," started Thompson, "we hadn't done much of anything for the past couple of years. Everything just seemed to be a dead end. Now and then, we'd look through all of our stuff and just couldn't think of anything to do next." Thompson wasn't saying much of anything, but his arms waved as if he was a prophet proclaiming the arrival of the next Messiah. "But we still kept up with all the news. We watched your film, you know, trying to see if anyone else was coming up with anything new. And after we had dinner with you guys in Boston, we were determined to get back in it. We made a list of everyone that might have been involved, trying to find any loose end that might lead us back on the trail. Pete came up with the idea of re-doing all the interviews again." Thompson nodded and waved wildly at Pete, who came to life.

"Well," Pete began, "a good detective always checks and rechecks with his witnesses. That's how they do it in the movies, right? Every time something new comes to light, he wants to get everyone's reaction to it." Pete's full head of jet-black hair, greying slightly at the temples and ears, nodded left and right as he spoke. He used his hands too, but unlike Thompson, he always kept them close to his chest like he was holding a box of something precious. "Most of these people, we hadn't talked to since '03. I still have all the cassette tapes, though."

Josh perked up. "We need to digitize those," he said. "I'll get you the name of a local company that does it, and they can bill me... as long as you're okay with us using them. We'll have to get releases from the interviewees also."

"Sure, that's no problem," said Pete, looking over to Thompson for confirmation. "So the first name we thought of was Bob Kessler, you know, the jock who interviewed Bernie—Bernie Lindstrom, that was the name of the security guard from Logan." Pete shifted in his seat a bit, sitting up straighter now. "Bob said don't bother to come, that he didn't remember anything that would help us. Of course, we wanted to come anyway, but he suggested checking with Lindstrom's wife first. Then we realized we hadn't spoken to her since he died."

Thompson jumped back in, holding both hands out in front of him in the 'stop' position and shaking his head. "She hadn't said word one when we first met with Bernie. And you don't like to bring up the past when someone's trying to get over the death of a loved one. But it's been six, seven years now." He paused for effect. Josh held his chin in one hand and nodded as he listened. "Ava—"

"That's the wife?" Josh asked.

"That's Bernie's wife," Thompson answered. "She told us things that didn't even come up back then with Bernie. It seems that after the interview with Kessler, he had more time to think. He had been scheduled off Wednesday and Thursday—

the 12th and 13th—and, of course, there were no flights. But there were all these people stuck at the airport, and his supervisor told Bernie he would probably be called in for extra help and new procedures.

"This kind of stuff was going on all over the country when most people were at home glued to pictures of a smoking Manhattan on the TV. But at Logan, it was especially crazy. She said he had called her Wednesday morning to tell her about it. Boston Police, FBI, Customs, everybody was there, all shifts. They had him helping out with the passengers. I think the local diocese or someone had provided food, and he was handing out sandwiches and pop. He answered questions, got the EMTs for an older lady that was short of breath. You know, they didn't have the TSA back then. Airport security was more like a rent-a-cop job anyway.

"When Bernie came home late that night," Thompson continued, "he had had to take the last train out, and she picked him up at Worcester at close to midnight. He was tired, but they stayed up another three hours talking about what had happened that day." Thompson had settled down a bit and was not moving his arms as much, but his eyes betrayed the intensity of a man who had been mining gold his whole life and had finally found a massive nugget on his claim.

"Good, good," said Josh. "You got this all on tape again?"

"*Oh* yeah," Pete chimed in. "Go ahead, John."

Thompson took a deep breath. "Like I said, they had him doing little things, helping out, but it wasn't his shift, so he didn't have any real place to be. So he spent a lot of time hanging around the security operations center."

"What's that, like the main office or something?" Josh inquired.

"No," Thompson replied, "it was really where they had guys watching security monitors." Thompson adjusted his glasses and pulled up a sheet of his notes.

"We're pretty sure it doesn't exist anymore," said Pete. "They built a new state-of-the-art center that takes up a whole building, completed a couple years ago."

"Anyway, he's hanging out there," Thompson continued, "drinking coffee and discussing what was going on. Now, since that time, like Pete said, Logan has practically been rebuilt, especially in terms of security. Hundreds of millions of dollars, a thousand new cameras, full-body scanners. But even then, security was pretty tight. The main security areas were monitored and recorded. After the previous day and night, Bernie wanted to find out about those passengers he had escorted to an empty room in the terminal.

"Bernie went to the video library. I'm not sure, but it was probably right next to the ops center, or even in a part of the same room. We need to get with some old-timers and nail this stuff down. Anyway, Ava says he saw all the tapes from the eleventh right there on the shelf. He looked through them, found the one for the terminal he had worked in, and played it. Sure enough, he and his train of passengers were on the tape. Maybe the crew was with them, she didn't know, and Bernie might not have remembered either."

"What happened to that tape?"

"There's the rub," said Pete.

"There's the rub," said Thompson.

"What's the rub?" asked Josh.

"The rub," said Pete, "is that we don't know. We do know that Bernie put it back on the shelf that day and that he never removed it or copied it or looked for it again."

"So, we still have lots of questions to answer." Josh was excited and disappointed at the same time. And tired.

"Sure," said Pete. "What was their retention policy? Did they follow it regarding the 9/11 tapes?"

"Did anybody make a copy on the eleventh? Surely they were reviewed at some point," said Thompson.

"And if they did survive," Josh chimed, "what happened to them when they switched over to the new system, which presumably was DVR-based? Tell me one thing, guys. What made Bernie want to call up the radio station in the first place? Sure, it was unusual to pull a whole planeload of people off and put them in a room, separated. But he had been through a lot that day. Why did he think it was newsworthy?"

Thompson and Pete looked at each other and smiled. Pete said, "You mean we haven't told you yet?"

"No," Josh said wearily.

Thompson shook his head. "There's one thing of which we're absolutely certain. Bob Kessler confirmed it, Bernie Lindstrom confirmed it, and now Ava has confirmed it as well. According to Bernie, the flight he escorted those people off was American Airlines flight eleven."

"Right," said Josh. Did he already know that? "I think I need some sleep."

CHAPTER SEVENTEEN

BELTWAY

n the history of transportation, perhaps no greater test of one's patience could be found than the task of driving a few miles on the Capital Beltway between the hours of four and six any weekday afternoon. The interstate highway had initially been designed to bypass Washington DC traffic. But, despite widening to the point that there were twelve lanes of traffic, six on the Inner Loop and six on the Outer Loop, it continues to be among the most congested corridors nationwide. This is the quagmire in which Ty and Andreas found themselves.

After three hours of Ty driving, while Andreas reworked his notes and narrative based on the news about Julie, they had reached the northern border of Virginia, and the Beltway was the only way to get through the mass exodus from

DC to continue further on I-95. A vast sea of red taillights stretched out ahead, flanked by a similar band of white headlights to the left. Ty envisioned them as stripes in an enormous illuminated American flag. Fortunately, he still had his sense of humor. "Andy, can I call you Andy?"

"Why not," said Andreas. He could only stare at his laptop screen for so long in a moving vehicle.

"Do you think we'll have to pay taxes here if we stay long enough?" As he finished the question, he felt his phone vibrate in his pocket.

"I think the tags may expire too," Andreas quipped. "But they'll have to send bicycle cops out to ticket us. They'd never get to us in a cruiser."

"Well, that's good 'cause I think we're going to need to switch seats. Unless you want to do some deciphering." Ty had received a short, simple text message on his phone that read simply: "Go message." This was code meaning a new post was available on a secret blog.

"I can probably handle that better than I can handle swapping seats in a quasi-moving vehicle," said Andreas, looking at Ty's phone.

"Okay. You'll need my laptop. It's either in my backpack or lying on the back seat." The older man turned around, grabbed the laptop, and started booting it, simultaneously closing his and swapping the power cord from one to the other. "I have the site bookmarked, and I don't have the URL memorized. If I'd known *this* situation would come up, I would have learned it or put it on my phone or something. Anyway, you'll also need a book from my backpack."

Andreas looked around some more, finally producing a paperback copy of Steven King's *11/22/63*. "Got it."

"That's the key text," Ty explained. "The message is on a blog. One of my bookmarks says 'Josh's blog' or something like that."

"I'm there, but..." Andreas was looking at a completely white page.

"But it looks blank?" Ty said. "Actually, the text is the same color as the background. Just paste the whole page into a new plain text document."

Andreas shook his head. "Cloak and dagger. Okay. It looks pretty long. What's the format?"

"Well, it really is a blog, so you only need the latest post. Once you isolate that, it's page, then line, then letter. That's why it's so long. But if you use words instead of letters, there are always some you can't find."

Andreas had isolated the message, and this is what he saw:

  10.1.3,10.1.4,10.5.1,10.5.12,9.1.3,9.15.2,
  9.1.8,9.9.3,12.5.8,12.2.4,

845.1.1,474.23.4,828.29.2,45.10.20,19

5.4.1,225.10.1,477.1.16,57.10.4,587.4.

7,534.3.41,

166.33.36,199.1.4,62.4.15,3.22.6,256.23.4

"Chapter titles don't count, punctuation doesn't count," Ty added.

"Got it. Just let me work." Andreas had to work with a flashlight in his mouth, the book in one hand, and the laptop balanced on his lap. After a few minutes, he had finished. "It says GoSpringfieldMASeussMotel."

Ty furrowed his brow. "Masseuse?"

"Well, there are some capitals," said Andreas. "Looks like M-A for Massachusetts."

"Good work, Andy. I guess we're headed northeast instead of northwest." Ty was trying to get over into the next lane as their exit was coming up.

"Wonder why?" Andreas was slumped in the seat, relaxing after contorting himself with the flashlight, book, and laptop.

"Did Jake ever tell you about the Bay State Boys?" Ty waved to the driver behind him in thanks as he eased into the next lane to his right. "That's what I call them anyway. We had dinner with them one night at *TruthCon* up in Boston."

"Sure," Andreas replied. "Before this Toronto thing, they were our biggest next lead. I wasn't sure it would pan out into anything, though. This message was from Josh, right?"

"I'm assuming it was. But since this is how we are all communicating now, it could have come from Jake."

"Who sent the text?" asked Andreas.

"I get an automatic text whenever one of us adds a new post to the site. Not sure what it means, I guess we'll find out when we get there at..." Ty looked at his watch. "...well, one or two in the morning."

"Well, let me know if you need me to drive for a while. I don't think I can do any more work tonight." Andreas had put all the gear behind him again and shifted down in his seat as he gazed out the window at the Maryland night going by.

CHAPTER EIGHTEEN

TORONTO

It was very early. Streetlights still glowed but had almost finished their duties for the night. Treetops were visible in the parks and medians, but darkness filled the spaces between the leaves. It was beautiful and almost quiet. It was about as quiet as downtown Toronto ever was. The sparse traffic mainly consisted of taxicabs, which lined up at the high-rise office buildings to collect business travelers bound for Toronto Pearson International Airport and then to New York, London, or Hong Kong. Buses and streetcars, absent now, were somewhere warming up their engines or electric motors.

Liam, disheveled and uniformed, emerged from the Norwich Coffee Shop in the middle of the block. He held a broom in one hand, a cigarette in the other. Liam looked neither left nor right at first, just put the cigarette in his mouth and began searching his pockets for a light. He was in no hurry. He patted his front pants pockets. He patted his back pants pockets. He patted the breast pocket of his uniform smock. Finally, he reached into one of the front pockets of his pants and pulled out a gold Zippo. He lit the cigarette that was still hanging from his mouth and took a long pull on it. He looked straight across the street at the gray figure sitting on a bus stop bench, one leg stretched out on it, a backpack between its legs.

Very few cars were parked on the non-residential block a hundred yards away, but Liam could see one black Chevy Caprice waiting near a corner. Inside, a clean-cut man lowered the driver's side window. His face said he didn't want to leave the vehicle but thought he might need to.

Jacob looked intently into the front of the lens of his Nikon. In his other hand, he held a small swath of cloth. After moving the camera back and forth until it reflected some light, he saw his image looking back. Satisfied, he stuffed the rag into one of the pockets on his backpack, raised the viewfinder to his eye, and began scanning the area, looking for something worth shooting.

Jacob wasn't much of an artistic photographer, but there were always times during "stakeouts" like this one when there wasn't anything to do but wait until his subject appeared. He had the camera, so he looked for a way to use it.

Unfortunately, by then, he was blind to much of this environment, having spent many hours here. He remembered seeing a documentary about a photographer who shot the same tree every day. It was right there on his property, right outside his door. And yet, he found it an interesting enough subject to capture it thousands of times. There were pictures of the tree in winter, bare of leaves, with snow piled on the limbs. There were pictures of it in heavy winds, bent almost to the breaking point. Others showed water dripping from the branches. Others showed it washed out in sunlight at high noon. Jacob remembered the man was in his seventies or eighties. Perhaps he would have that kind of patience and eye for things when he was older. For now, it was hard to imagine. Still, sunrise was a great time to shoot almost anywhere. He clicked off a shot of a fire escape whose shadows were just becoming visible. It was going to be a long day.

Liam held his cigarette between two fingers as he gripped the broom and turned to his left. Looking straight at the clean-cut man in the Chevy, he nodded. The man nodded back, started the car, and drove away. Liam was opening today, part of the extra hours he had requested, and that Bob had gladly given him. If Bob were here, he would probably offer a reminder that smoking was illegal, well, anywhere in the city except private homes. But Liam was alone now. Bob wouldn't be in until the morning rush started. Within the hour, he could expect one of the cashiers to show up. Liam stepped on his cigarette butt, then picked it up and walked inside to check the espresso machines. The kid wasn't going anywhere.

Watching dawn turn into day was an experience that had a similar, somewhat magical quality, no matter where one experienced it. It wasn't really possible to see the change until blinking or turning one's head. Jacob sat alone on his bench. No one else was in sight on that block. Two people walked out of a consulting firm office to separate taxis. Four cars arrived at a stoplight. Eight people exited a bus that had just arrived. A constant stream of suited and tied workers passed before his eyes. A pack of commuters squeezed past each other, half of them entering the coffee shop. The coffee shop! Realizing it was now rush hour, Jacob shouldered his pack. Nikon on a strap on the other shoulder, he hurried to the crosswalk to position himself where he had seen Julie the first time. He felt the familiar rush of adrenaline in expectation of achieving his goal. Intellectually, logically, he knew Julie might not even be in the city anymore, but his hopes were high despite this. He didn't want to confront her yet, especially right there in the street. He planned to wait in the coffee shop so he wouldn't be seen, then try to find out where she worked, so he could tailor his approach to the environment and devise a way to meet her alone and give her the pitch.

That was the plan, but things didn't go as planned. As soon as he entered the crosswalk, Jacob saw Julie coming straight for him. Shocked, he looked directly at her for a microsecond. Somehow he regained his wits, looked away and down, and glided out of her path. When he had crossed the street, he waited a few seconds, then turned around, scanning the thickening crowd for the shoulder-length jet-black hair he had studied for hours in those nine exposures from his last trip here. He spotted her walking at a brisk pace back up the block toward the bus stop. The light had already changed, so he moved up the block on his side of the street. He passed Norwich Coffee. She walked past the bus stop. Jacob stayed back and made sure not to stare in case she looked in his direction. He expected her to continue across the next street into the next block.

Liam tamped out a double espresso for a stunning blonde in a light grey pinstripe suit. Though it was hard to see from this vantage point, Liam knew exactly where Jacob was. He watched the familiar camera backpack trot past the front window. Liam assumed Jacob would continue either looking for or actually following Julie Foley to her office at Emerald Financial, a block and a half away. One or both of them would be back, and he could do his job and hopefully collect a cool ten grand. Either that, or he'd receive more instructions, and the price would increase.

Liam would prefer that his involvement in whatever problems this woman had were ended sooner rather than later. Along with the increased payoff came increased risk and the possibility of exposure, and Liam did not want anyone knowing enough about him to hold a grudge.

Plenty of NSA assets had disappeared in such situations, or so he had heard. He would just move on to whatever was next in his life. But for now, the job wasn't finished. He capped the cup. "Ashley? Naked double?" He placed the drink into her manicured fingers, offering a subdued, closed-lipped smile.

The next morning, Jacob waited in Julie's building. He had learned that it was much easier to conceal that he was following someone if he was already at the destination when the person arrived. There was no need to tail Julie when Jacob knew where she was going to be. He was wearing coveralls and a cap. He had toyed with the idea of strapping on a tool belt but figured it would be out of place if he were supposed to be part of the morning rush coming into the building. Today, his mission was not to confront her but merely to find out exactly where she worked and what gatekeepers he had to navigate to see her in person the next day. He had already checked the building directories and found no one named Julie Foley, which was hardly surprising since she was supposed to be dead.

He spotted Julie through the windows that spanned the entire front wall of the lobby. Time to go. He moved toward the elevators, then located his target in his peripheral vision. He had only one chance to time this right. Only five people were standing in the lobby. All would go on the next elevator. As the doors opened to an empty elevator, Jacob jumped in first and moved to the back. Julie and the others moved in and turned to face the front. She was quite attractive in a girl-next-door kind of way. He heard her voice for the first time as she asked for her floor. Not enough to catch an accent. She was supposed to be from a small Arkansas town. She was educated, though, and had seen much of the world during her years as a flight attendant. So it was very possible that she could blend in here. Not only were the differences in inflection subtle, but there was a lot of moving back and forth between Toronto and Detroit and other cities in the Great Lakes area. Natives might easily mistake an Arkansas accent for rural Ohio.

After dropping off one passenger on the third floor, the car went all the way to the tenth and top level. Jacob waited until all of the others had gotten off, and the doors started to close; then, he stuck his arm between the doors to stop them. Julie was just entering the front door of Emerald Financial, straight ahead. As the door closed, he quickly walked to it, then opened it slowly. Julie was gone. There was a receptionist. He had to act fast.

"Excuse me," Jacob said, walking up to the reception desk. The girl there apparently had just recently arrived herself. Her purse was in the middle of her desk. She was standing, turning on a flat-screen TV mounted on the wall behind the desk.

"Can I help you?" she asked, pulling out her chair and stowing her purse in the bottom right drawer of her desk.

"Yes, uh, do you know who that lady was that just came through here?" Jacob asked. "About thirty, she had shoulder-length black hair." He was putting on his most innocent, most helpful face and trying to act as if he worked in the building, but was seldom in a front office such as this one and was more comfortable in the basement or up on the roof tinkering with cooling units or something.

"Why, you like her?" The girl smiled, cheerful for this time of the morning. Jacob supposed she had a beau herself. He smiled back and pulled a dollar bill out of his pocket.

"I don't know about that," he said with a chuckle. "But I think she might be the one that dropped this." He held up the dollar. "I found it in the elevator, and she was just leaving."

"Well, that's Emily Martin," said the receptionist. "She's an account manager/financial planner. Want me to get her for you?" She put her hand on the phone.

"On second thought, why don't you just give it to her? I'm late for a date with a heat pump upstairs."

"Okay," she said, taking the dollar.

Jacob walked out, thinking his next move might be a bit more difficult. The receptionist would probably recognize him if she saw him again anytime soon.

CHAPTER NINETEEN

GREEN EGGS AND HAM

Three raised arms waved from side to side at a corner table as Josh and Ty walked through the aluminum-framed glass doors of Green Eggs & Ham, the restaurant at the Seuss Motel. They looked at each other and shook their heads. Nodding to the hostess and pointing to the table, they made their way to the large circular table and sat down. John and Pete were smiling, as was Andreas. They already had coffee in front of them and were apparently having a good time.

"Well, I guess you guys know each other," said Josh. Andreas had not met the Bay State Boys before. "Didn't we say seven o'clock?" He and Ty both indicated to the waitress that they wanted coffee.

"When you become an old fart like us, you'll be up early, too," laughed Pete. Ty, leaning back in his chair and tapping his fingers on the vinyl-covered art deco table, grinned at Andreas.

The waitress set a pot of steaming coffee on the table and put cups in front of Ty and Josh. "Ready to order?" She looked at the two filmmakers. The other three had already placed their order.

"When in Rome, Mr. Kitt?" Josh said to Ty.

"Do as Romans do, Mr. Wynn," Ty responded, then looked up at the waitress, who was standing almost directly behind him. "Green eggs and ham."

She looked at Josh. "Same," said Josh.

"Diamonds Ah Forevah!" said Pete, picking up on the reference.

"Bond ... Josh Bond," Josh responded, in his best Sean Connery voice. "So," he said seriously, "what did we miss?"

"Nothing," said Andreas. "We were just getting to know each other. The meeting hasn't officially started."

"The main reason I wanted to meet up was to get some input from Ty and everyone else on what should happen next," Josh began. "But I'm glad you two got to meet Andreas. You've been working on this angle for a long time separately. So now you can compare notes. This is officially a Freefall Productions film project. Our company is funding all this travel and other expenses, and we need to work this angle somehow while Jacob is making contact and, if we're very lucky, getting an interview. If he does, this thing's going to drop like a nuclear bomb." He put some cream into his coffee and stirred it.

"But," Josh continued, "if she's all there is, there will still be a lot of skeptics. They'll say she never boarded the flight, ran away, the whole bit. It's like Hitler said: the bigger the lie, the more they believe it. That's why your thing," he pointed his two index fingers at Thompson and Pete, "especially the security tapes or any kind of physical evidence, is so important. Plus, if he doesn't get her on video, it will be the only real evidence we have." Josh took a drink of his coffee and looked at Andreas as if to challenge him.

"Well," offered Andreas, "I know the basic story you guys told Jake. What else is—?"

"And," Josh interrupted, continuing to look straight at Andreas, "if there *is* an interview up North, I want *you* to ask the questions. You're the expert. Here's the decision I need to make now. Jake's producing the Toronto segment. Ty will shoot these guys and their contacts here. You're the principal writer on this film. Where do you need to be right now? Just think about it. John, why don't you guys give Andreas the quick and dirty? Bring him up to date."

As Thompson started, breakfast appeared in front of Josh. He looked at the two dyed, fried eggs, toast, and a slice of ham in front of him. In a way, Josh felt at peace, though this was ironic in what appeared to be chaos all around him. But, he thought, that's the business. It's not nine-to-five. And finally, he felt at home, in his rightful place at the helm of a growing, maturing project, delegating production to known competent and creative professionals, wrangling subject matter experts that had never worked on a real film before, bringing out the true talents of those around him. Making the crucial decisions could mean the difference between a solid, significant project and a hacked-up hit piece.

After a few minutes, Andreas was filled in and ready to work. "Josh, I think we have a couple of options. I can work here, write up what we have from the tapes and what I've just heard, fleshing out details, and putting together the interview questions. I'd like to be there when we record the wife. What was her name? Ava. I have a few ideas on finding that tape too. That way, when Jake confirms the interview, I can just drive up there. I already have a question list for her that I put together on the drive up." Pete and Thompson nodded along, picking at their breakfast.

"But will you be there in time?" Josh knew that Julie was the biggest unknown in this grand equation. She could rabbit, or dig in and hole up, or just say no, or call the cops, or call somebody else he hadn't thought of. There was no way to know, and the best weapon against the unknown was to prepare for anything.

"Good point," said Andreas. "I could also leave a couple of tips here, go north, and keep in touch with the blog."

"The blog isn't good for strategy or discussion," Josh said. "Takes too long to decode. We just use it for the shortest and most urgent communications."

"What if we used an unlikely link?" said Pete. "I got a nephew who deals poker up there."

"Not with a cell phone or email," said Josh.

"Fax over a landline?"

"Not if it's in a public place," Josh said, shaking his head. "Look, when I compared this thing to a nuclear bomb, I mean it was *that* impactful. This information can't come out before our press conference. And that can't come until we get Julie's interview in the can." Josh looked out the window. After all the options were processed in his brain, the result was clear. "It's a day's drive to Toronto. Until we finish one or the other of these segments, I'm going to have to be the shuttle." He looked at Ty. "Unless there's someone else we can trust."

Ty knew of two. "Steve or Michaelyn," he offered, "but I think they both have jobs."

"Let's call 'em and see," Josh ordered with a *What have we got to lose?* look. "When our investor comes through, we need to bring someone else in anyway. We need to cover Cleveland too, and the quicker this all gets done, the better chance we have of meeting budget. After that, I can put them on a new project—it's expand or die these days. We almost ran out of cash, waiting for this thing."

The waitress was picking up the dirty plates. "How 'bout some more coffee?" she said with a smile.

"How 'bout them Pats?" Josh asked cheerfully. "Yeah, I think we'll need some more here."

"They're doin' real good this year. Okay, I'll bring another pot." Pete was getting a newspaper. Ty was in the bathroom. The meeting was loosening up.

"Brady and Belichick. Hard to beat that combo." Thompson was displaying his New England pride.

"You know," said Josh, "I envy Brady's looks, money, and fame. But I'd trade all of that not to have that bum knee the rest of my life."

"Nothing comes free," said Andreas. "Especially if you want to be famous." He said it as one who had no such desires.

"Yeah. It's important *why* you're famous," Josh said as one who did have such desires.

Josh had taken a lot of criticism for his films. Although he was one of four producers on the first *Freefall*, he had always been the most outspoken of the group, and he rarely turned down an interview or an opportunity to promote them.

He thought over his career thus far. People, in general, didn't want to believe there might be kinks in the official story of 9/11. It was much easier to think a bunch of Saudis trained in Afghanistan, sponsored by an already-famous and wealthy radical Muslim, then snuck into the country, cleverly hijacking four airliners and smashing them kamikaze-style into symbolic targets. All done without any help from the West, of course. Institutional journalists had vested interests in maintaining the status quo and didn't want to upset their main contributors. So, Josh and company examined the facts with fine-toothed combs and brought out every discrepancy in interviews through the years. The sequel was an effort to counteract the bad press by answering some of those tough questions and correcting and clarifying statements made in the original film. Not that any of the criticism hurt the popularity of the films. Fame was a double-edged sword, but it had its advantages.

Ty was walking back, turning off his phone. "Steve has to work," he reported. "Michaelyn substitute teaches. Says she can take a couple of weeks off."

"Wants to help?" Josh considered the responsibility. He felt it keenly for each of his team members, and even more now with a new and inexperienced person joining up.

"She wants to help." Ty looked around and turned his coffee cup bottoms up. "We need to get moving. Daylight's precious."

Josh picked up the check as they all rose and walked toward the cashier and the door of Green Eggs & Ham. "Okay, I'll contact her and get her moving this way. Get your gear, take these guys, and get Ava's interview in the can A.S.A.P. I'll be at the hotel to bring Michaelyn up to speed as soon as I make one stop."

"What for?" Ty asked.

"Let's just say Stephen King's going to sell another copy of his latest book."

CHAPTER TWENTY

EMILY MARTIN

He didn't quite look like a high-income professional but more like an intern or a somewhat conservative student. Jacob did not approve of the man looking back at him in the mirror. In order to blend in enough not to scare folks in the front office of Emerald Financial, he calculated that his best option was to dress like an engineer. Jacob looked too young to be a convincing doctor or dentist, and a lawyer would be expected to handle his own investments. He had put on chinos and a long-sleeve polo shirt. Something wasn't right, and it was just hanging out there.

Grasping a fresh coffee from the single-cup brewer in his hotel room, Jacob gazed out the window at Toronto, glaring in the late morning sun. The TV was tuned to a news channel to give him perspective and to keep him from going nuts listening to the sound of his own thoughts.

"...*and leaders of three major political parties have now taken some sort of credit for or made some statement of support for Occupy Toronto. Here's Bob with sports. Bob, looks like the Raptors are going to have a season after all, eh?*"

Jacob went through the approach in his head. Straightforward but not straight-on was the approach he had decided on. Tell the truth, but not until you can tell the whole truth. Get into her office, close the door, and *then* go for it. He shook his head, then went to the unslept-in second bed in his room, which was covered entirely in clothes: shoes, belts, ties, socks. There were many different colors and all styles, from super-casual to semi-formal. He reached across the head of the bed and picked up a dark brown sweater, unfolded it, and examined it. He felt the texture. Pulling it on over his polo shirt, he went back to the mirror. "Oh yeah," he said. "Hello, mister engineer." But he remembered the receptionist. If there was more time, he would get a haircut. What else could he do? He went back to the array on the bed. He had a number of accessories in one of those self-evacuating space-saver plastic bags: a headband, clip-on bowtie, various watches. He put on a Casio diver's watch and picked up a pair of horn-rimmed glasses.

Rechecking himself in the mirror, he determined that he might get by the receptionist, but he would try to avoid her this time.

Of course, he had the option of doing more surveillance. He was basically on his own here. But time is money. It was a delicate balance. If he didn't take enough time, he might not get an interview or even any information. If he took too much time, the movie might lose money, or he might arrive home at his apartment to find an eviction notice and a padlock on the door for nonpayment of rent. He looked at the clock. It was almost eleven a.m. He knew there were several administrative assistants at Emerald who filled in for the receptionist at lunchtime. But he didn't know what Julie's lunchtime habits were. He decided to try to make an appointment for early afternoon. When he called, the receptionist he had seen earlier answered.

"Hello, this is Troy Jones," Jacob began. "I was wondering if I could get in to see Emily Martin this afternoon. I got a good report on her from an acquaintance, and I'm considering placing some of my non-retirement funds under management." The problem with using his real name was that the first thing someone does when meeting someone new is to run an internet search. He counteracted this by doing a preemptive search and strategically choosing an appropriate result. Now when Julie threw Troy Jones on a search engine, she would find a mild-mannered engineering resume and a Facebook page with no picture and sparse details. At this point, he hoped she did look him up, so she would feel comfortable and off-guard.

"I'm sorry, she's got a full schedule today," the receptionist replied. "I have a nine a.m. tomorrow?"

Jacob persisted, "Can you check with her about squeezing me in somewhere? I'm going out of town tomorrow, and I wanted to get started on this before the next tax year." Jacob sat down on the edge of the "disguise" bed, looking out the window.

"Just a moment." As the receptionist switched to hold to check with Julie, Jacob sipped his coffee and tried to think of alternatives. Tomorrow morning wouldn't be too bad, but he'd already gambled that away by saying he was going out of town. Just then, he heard a different voice on the phone.

"Mister Jones? I'm Emily Martin." Jacob tried to gather his wits. She sounded confident and secure—not like a victim at all. For a moment, he doubted his whole theory. Then he remembered the photographs. His eyes had not lied to him.

"Hello!" he chirped. "Sorry to interrupt you, I just have a tight schedule, and I was putting this off until I found someone by word of mouth. Do you understand?" Jacob tried to keep his voice from trembling. He had spoken with former presidents and billionaires with no trouble at all, but this was different. Julie was so much more important.

"Uh, yeah, I guess so. If we have a cancellation, I can fit you in. I just wish you could have called earlier."

"Are you available now?" He was just a few blocks away.

"For about twenty minutes. But that doesn't give us much time to discuss your needs. Um..." Julie seemed very nice. Jacob hated to push her, but time was of the essence. "Tell you what. I will grab a sandwich, and you can stop by during lunch. That okay?"

"Thanks, I really appreciate it," Jacob said.

"Around noon, then?"

As he hung up, Jacob stood and looked around the room. Final preparations were in order, and he needed to go through all of the points he *had* to make in this meeting. Jacob wasn't a kidnapper. He had to convince her that he knew who she was and be ready to help her. He also had to be prepared if she decided not to cooperate. Jacob sat down at the desk and picked up a hotel pen and some stationery. Physically writing seemed to help his mind work sometimes.

But his list would have to wait. He heard his phone rattle on one of the bedside tables across the room. He had left it set on vibrate. It only rattled once. Another coded message had come in. He set aside the stationery and went to his laptop to retrieve the encrypted blog entry. He decoded the brief message quickly:

MICHAELYN EN RT TORONTO
KNOWS CODE

Good. Jacob could use a little help now. He encoded a message with the hotel info, blogged it, and sent her a text. He would leave a key for her at the front desk.

By the time he had finished with the communications, it was time to leave for his appointment. He checked himself once more in the mirror, grabbed a folder full of fake financial documents, and walked quickly out the door.

Jacob, now sweatered, bespectacled, slightly hunching over, loped toward the receptionist, trying to be, as much as possible, the opposite of his alter-ego maintenance man of the day before. He had hoped to be there during a lunch break, but he had little choice or time to research break times. She was on the phone, and he patiently waited until she finished making another appointment.

"Whew! I haven't even had time for lunch." She looked at Jacob expectantly.

"Ah, Troy Jones to see Emily Martin," Jacob said. He glanced toward her monitor, trying to influence her to focus somewhere other than his face.

"She's usually at lun—. Oh, I remember now. You called this morning. I'll tell her you're here."

Julie walked toward him in dark blue pants, heels, and a white-and-blue striped button-down shirt open at the collar. She looked slightly casual for a financial services office, and he imagined she had removed a matching jacket during lunch and left it in her office. She extended her hand. "Emily Martin," she said with a firm grip.

"Troy Jones," Jacob returned. He followed her the short distance down a hallway perpendicular to the entrance hall and around the corner to her office. It was small, but had a nice view, overlooking the park where he had spent so much time. It made him think of this whole trip at a higher level, literally and figuratively.

Julie brought him quickly back to business. "Would you like some coffee?" she asked, closing the door behind him.

"No thanks," he said, easing toward a chair in front of her L-shaped desk. On the walls were a couple of pictures of foreign places: Paris, Greece—nothing personal or unique.

A University of Michigan diploma and Certified Financial Planner certificate hung on the wall behind her.

"So I understand you have some discretionary funds you'd like to invest," Julie asked. She was very patient with him, even though he had taken her lunch hour. The woman was very good at this job and seemed a bit more relaxed and friendly on her own turf. In the street, her guard was up. Jacob considered Julie's experience as a flight attendant, all the travel. She had seen the world and experienced the people in it. Neither naïve nor reclusive, Julie was, in fact, a very well-balanced person. He looked into her eyes for some indication as to how he should proceed. He could see nothing. It didn't matter. Now was the time to act.

"Listen. I didn't come here to talk about investing. I know who you are." Jacob had set down the folder of documents, removed his fake glasses, and leaned forward in his chair.

Julie laughed. "I give up, Mr. Jones," she said in a playful, disarming way. "Who am I?"

Jacob tried to put a look of understanding friendship on his face. "You're Julie Foley, former flight attendant for American Airlines." The smile drained from Julie's face, and traces of worry replaced it. "I'm a journalist, and my real name is Jacob. I want to hear your story."

"You're crazy," she said, looking left and right, seemingly trapped in the small office behind the desk, ten floors up. "I think you should leave." She glanced at the phone.

"Okay," Jacob said in his most reassuring voice, "but I really want to speak with you. My information is in the folder, along with a place where I'll be if you decide to meet me." He stood up slowly and backed toward the door as Julie bit a nail and continued to shift her focus around the walls of her office.

As he was almost out the door, he heard her voice behind him. "Wait a minute," she said, a slight Arkansas twang slipping into her speech. He turned around. She had opened the folder and glanced at it. "I know this place," Julie said. He nodded. Then she said, "Five-thirty today." He wanted to ask if she was okay, but he could tell she was more worried about him being there than anything else. He put his fake glasses on, turned, and walked back down the hallway. He smiled as he approached the receptionist, who was now eating some chips at her desk.

"That was quick," said the receptionist. "Do you need to make another appointment?" She looked slightly concerned and wasn't smiling back.

"No," said Jacob. "I'll call, thanks." He tried to put on his hunched lope again as he moved toward the elevator. As he turned around and pushed the lobby button, he exhaled in relief. He had made contact. There was no turning back. He felt for Julie and hoped she wasn't so scared that she would do something drastic. He probably should keep an eye on her. Then again, he should also get mobile, pack up his gear, and prepare to move. After all, she had made a date. If only Michaelyn were already here.

CHAPTER TWENTY-ONE

MICHAELYN

She had long, light-brown hair worn in a ponytail, stylish clear-frame glasses, and pink lip gloss. She wore a pink, long-sleeve pullover blouse over jeans. The heater was blasting, and a fur-lined winter coat lay on the passenger seat beside her, along with a smartphone and a netbook computer. Michaelyn was hurling down the Masspike at ninety miles an hour. She passed a white sedan that looked like a police car and noticed how fast she was going. As she slowed and moved to the right lane, Michaelyn reached for the radio and turned the old plastic dial until some music came on that was relatively unmolested by static. Then she leaned back, more relaxed, with one hand on the thin steering wheel and an elbow propped on the armrest of the driver side door.

She drove a light blue 1968 Mustang she had bought when she was in high school. It broke down a lot, but she would never give it up. She loved to feel the vibration as she pushed the gas pedal to the floor. It was familiar. It was exhilarating. The car was not one of the more powerful versions available, but to her, it was an original muscle car, far more fun than any newer model she might be able to afford. There was always something else to do when she had extra money, something to replace or service. When she didn't have money, it was nice not to have a car payment.

Michaelyn didn't know what she would be asked to do on this trip—Josh had been pretty vague—but she wasn't afraid. She knew her husband's friends' hearts were in the right place. She had a sense about such things. It was too bad that Steve couldn't make it. She would miss him. But she felt that she was needed and was looking for an adventure, or at least a slight diversion. The monotony of teaching and home life had made her restless in the last few months. And though she wasn't jealous of Steve's occasional trips with Jacob, she needed to get away too. There was no telling how long these freedoms would be available since she knew they would decide to have children sometime soon. For now, she relished the open road. Five hours down, four to go.

CHAPTER TWENTY-TWO

AVA LINDSTROM

The room had a hushed and serious tone. Everyone seemed to have clarity about his or her purpose for being there. It was the middle of the afternoon, but there was little sunlight in the room. Ty had shut the blinds for more control over the lighting, even though some large trees in the front yard prevented any direct sunlight from coming into the living room. There was a slight smell of heating oil. Andreas did not recognize it. Pete and Thompson knew it was probably from a minor spill during pre-winter fuel delivery, a routine at this time of year for most residents. The grey carpet was starting to show wear, but the couple had furnished the room with relatively new leather furniture in light pastel colors. On one wall was a large crucifix, on the other an eight-by-ten photo of Ava and Bernie taken before 9/11, when they had only been married for a couple of years. There was also a smell of coffee coming from the kitchen. Ava had offered everyone a cup when they arrived.

She sat patiently in a stuffed armchair leaning on one armrest with her chin in her hand. Her knees were together, and her feet were crossed. She was peaceful, but there was a sadness about her face. She had short, brown hair, which hung straight, and she wore plenty of makeup, but not too much. She wore a white dress with a black pattern of flowers that appeared to be drawn in ink, flat canvas shoes, and a white cardigan sweater. Ava had not volunteered to do the interview, but she did not hesitate to agree when asked. She said it was the right thing to do and that she had never been at peace with Bernie's death. And that, like many people, neither of them had been the same since the morning of September 11, 2001.

Ava had not been available that morning due to a church function. While they waited, the team had made copies of Andreas's questions for everyone. They listened to the old interview tape for a couple of hours and hashed out the interview format. Thompson and Pete had a lot of input, and many of the questions from the previous interview would be repeated. But Josh had decided to make Andreas the chief interviewer here. In documentary films such as this, the interviewer would be off-screen, a narrator playing his role as clips from various interviews are spliced together to form a unified storyline. So the questions had to cover a wide range of topics, as the final storyline had not yet been written. Ty and Josh knew how this format worked and provided general guidance to the three researchers to put them on the right track.

At eye-level, slightly to her right, and across from her was a professional-model High-Definition video camera on a sturdy tripod. Cables from the camera were duct-taped to a leg of the tripod and floor. Immediately to the left of the camera sat Andreas, in a wooden chair brought from the kitchen. He sat with legs crossed and his notes in front of him, whispering to himself and making edits with a ballpoint pen. To his left was the couch, where Pete and Thompson sat, sipping coffee and casually looking through some notes as well.

Ty was moving from metal tree to metal tree, adjusting lighting angles, eliminating shadows, adding and subtracting artificial reflecting surfaces, and taking test shots with the camera. He had taken a couple of classes at a broadcasting school in between the two films he had worked on, but for the most part, he was self-taught. There were plenty of film and broadcasting schools and classes available in New York City, but there was no substitute for experience. When they started working full-time on the sequel, he dropped the classes since he was getting a far better education working with Josh on the film. While they still used a lot of news footage, their second effort included far more studio interviews. Through trial and error, Ty had learned how to make a solid interview film with a generic but clean look. A professional appearance was essential to capture the vital subject matter of the piece. If the production quality was substandard, it distracted the viewer from the subject, the whole reason they made the film in the first place.

"Almost ready," he said, stepping over a cable and walking around to his camera.

Andreas tried to make Ava as comfortable as possible. "As we discussed before," he said, "we'll spend the first few questions just talking about you and Bernie, how he came to work at the airport, things like that, just to establish the kind of person he was, mainly. Now, don't worry about what you say, or if you make a mistake, just keep on going, say as much as you like. It's better for us to have as much information to work with as possible because it will need to be condensed later. When you stop talking, we'll move on to the next question. Don't mention any of us when you're answering, but otherwise, just treat it like a normal conversation. Some of the questions you will have been asked before. It doesn't matter if you repeat yourself exactly. Just answer it based on what you know. If you want to take a break at any time, just let us know. We're in no hurry. Okay?" he smiled, and she smiled back and nodded.

Though Andreas was new to video, Ty knew Andreas had interviewed many people for his research, probably over the phone. But he was relaxed and confident. Andreas took a drink of water as Ty reframed for the last time. He would mostly have her in a half-shot, as she occasionally used her hands when speaking. But he would be standing by for a tighter close-up during more intense responses. "Whenever you're ready, Andy."

Andreas looked inquiringly at Ava, who nodded again and looked straight at him, ready to answer. "Describe when you first met Bernie and continue through the early years of your marriage."

Ava looked up, and a slight smile came to her face. "We lived in different towns but worked at the same McDonald's out on the Masspike. We were both in our senior year in high school." Ty was glad that Ava seemed a little happier now, reflecting on a happier time, but he also knew he had to concentrate and that it would be a long evening. They needed to get at least an hour here, hopefully, two or three. It was likely that less than ten percent of the footage would be used in the final film. The more they had to choose from, the better the final product would be. But he had spent the morning with these three guys hashing it out, and he was confident that Andreas would get what they needed.

"So, do you know anybody of consequence or means in Cleveland?" Josh was back at the Seuss, on the phone with Bill Sandusky. Now that Sandusky had come through with his funding, Josh considered him a partner of sorts and had no compunction asking for help if he thought the man could provide it.

"I may know a guy who knows a guy..." Sandusky quipped.

"I know what you're thinking!" Josh was in full Josh mode, exerting his personality into every challenge the day offered. Perhaps he had consumed too much coffee at breakfast. In retrospect, he thought it seemed a rather strong brew. "You're wondering what I could possibly need in Cleveland that would require means or consequence. And I'm going to tell you. You see, there are some people there that have decided it's too much bother to talk about what happened on 9/11. To relate their own unique experience of that day. I'm trying to help these people, Bill."

"Uh-huh. What kind of people?" Sandusky was playing along because he also knew that this partnership was real now. The money was gone, and it wasn't coming back unless this man succeeded. Whatever he needed in Cleveland, it was just as important to Bill as it was to Josh.

"So the mayor at the time made a few statements," Josh said. "He quickly retracted them. But the official story doesn't ring true. There are some problems with it. We want to confront him with these discrepancies. Not that he'll add any information to the story. What I'm looking for is flavor. The official denial. Then we go back and refute what he's saying with our other evidence." Josh was still hoping someone could just go to his house and get him to talk. "I understand he's a farmer now."

"Can't help ya, man," Sandusky said. "But I wish you all the luck in the world."

"Really?" Josh sounded disappointed.

"Yeah, nobody I know has any special history there. There's a distribution center nearby, of course, but it's not like we're a major employer, so politicians wouldn't be courting us."

"Okay, well, thanks anyway," Josh said earnestly. "And thanks for sending the money. Things are really moving now."

"I can see that." Sandusky smiled, and Josh knew it. They hung up the phone. Josh lay back on his bed and tried to think of what to do next.

"I don't remember how the tape was marked," Ava said. "Either he didn't say, or I just forgot. But I do know that there was only one tape for a whole day for each area." Ava recounted her 2001 conversation with Bernie with impressive clarity. It was obviously an important event in her life.

"Do you recall whether the recordings were multiplexed? That is, multiple cameras recorded on the same tape?" Andreas asked her.

"No, I don't, but Bernie did write some of this down. It might be in his notes. Have I shown you his journal?" Ava looked at John Thompson and over to Pete, though she had remembered not to say their names.

"We'll look it over," Pete assured her.

"It's a good time to take a break anyway," said Ty. They had been going for a couple of hours, and he wanted to shut down the gear for a while and let it and the room cool down. "So let's do that, relax for a while, and whenever you're ready, we'll take a look at this journal."

While the others milled around, stretching

their legs and making small talk, John Thompson came over to Ty, who was turning off each piece of gear. "I know it's important to get this interview done," said Thompson, "but I think I'm going to go look into something. There's a guy that used to work at Massport that was the project manager for the security revamping at Logan. He's moved on but still lives in Boston."

"It's getting late; will you still be able to see him?" Ty asked. "We'll be done here in an hour, I think. We won't need to come back tomorrow."

"He said I could drop by his house in Newton," said Thompson. "Thing is, he'll probably lead me to somewhere or someone else. He's not going to be a major figure like Ava, so it's probably not worth everyone showing up."

"Yeah," said Ty, flipping the switch on a tungsten light. "We need to find that tape. I agree. You should move on that."

"Okay, I'll just let the guys know," said Thompson.

"Let us know what?" Andreas was walking back into the room with a bottle of Moxie soda pop.

"I got a lead on the tape. I'm going to follow it while you guys are finishing up here," Thompson said, moving toward Ava to tell her goodbye.

"Moxie, huh?" Ty said to Andreas. "You like that stuff?"

"It's kind of interesting," Andreas commented. "Ava forced it on me when she found out I was from Virginia. She's really nice." He smiled.

"I don't know," Ty joked. "I hate that stuff. Could be she just doesn't like people from Virginia."

"We're almost done," Andreas said absently, looking for the ingredients on the label of the Moxie bottle.

"Yeah, I told John it wouldn't be more than an hour. But he didn't need us for his thing."

Andreas nodded.

"Looks like the bathroom's open." Ty walked away as Pete noticed the beverage.

"Don't drink too much Moxie, Andreas. It has 'special properties,'" laughed Pete. He was holding a fresh cup of coffee and making his way back to his spot on the couch.

"What do you mean?" Andreas grinned, looking at the bottle again. The jokes would always be on him in this crowd.

"Special," Pete said, sipping his coffee.

CHAPTER TWENTY-THREE

OCCUPIED

t was mid-afternoon in Toronto. The sun was out, but it didn't do much for the thirty-one-degree wind chill. Taxicab business was picking up. Fewer people walked on the sidewalks or through the grass in the park across from the Norwich Coffee Shop, where Liam stood looking out. He was bored, but he knew the photographer kid was still in town and assumed the girl was too. He hadn't delivered his message yet. His pocket buzzed as a customer walked in. He read the text as he followed the customer back toward his barista station:

MOVING TO YOU IN POV

It was from the other operative in his car. The man had been following Jacob while Liam waited for Julie to show up.

A few blocks away, Jacob sat in his rented Hyundai. Somehow, the heavy traffic, now at a standstill, was incredibly frustrating, even though he was in no hurry. He had nothing specific to do until his five-thirty date at the coffee shop, though he was second-guessing his decision not to stake out the office building in case his date was planning on standing him up.

Ahead at the intersection, police directed traffic, though no vehicle had moved in the last five minutes. Jacob could barely see a large group of people moving in front of the policemen and the tops of some signs and banners. It was some sort of protest parade. He turned on the radio and heard the last music station he had tuned to on the way into town several days earlier. He started scanning for news, then realized it was probably the last vestiges of the Occupy Wall Street movement, Toronto chapter. He was surprised it had survived this long into the cold weather and the school year. He tried to make out the lettering on the signs as the crowd continued to pass, noting the calm peacefulness of the whole thing.

Canadians were so nice to each other. In Manhattan, police had brutally beaten protesters, even though cameras were all over the event. They didn't even try to hide it. The same was true all over the States. He thought back to the tenth anniversary 9/11 memorial service. There was a police presence so thick you'd think it was a cop convention. The officials kept the protesters so far away they couldn't even see anyone involved in the event, the memorial, or any part of Ground Zero. Even first responders who were veterans of 9/11 were excluded from the service. Fortunately, there were few arrests or violent incidents, but only because of the overwhelming force involved. It was the rare case of the cops outnumbering the protesters.

But there was always violence involved in protest demonstrations, as long as Jacob could remember. He'd attended a number of them personally. There were always troublemakers among the protesters that didn't seem to belong. They would start the fights if the police didn't. Josh was always able to point them out. He said they were *agent provocateurs*. Jacob wondered why these guys didn't show up in places like Toronto.

There was no way to know what Julie had in mind. More likely than not, she didn't even know what she wanted to do, though, by the time they met that evening, she would have had time to think of something. Jacob was prepared for anything, though. He had checked out of the hotel and packed everything. The front desk said there were plenty of rooms available if he needed one later, but with this protest going, he wasn't sure of that. He had enough equipment to do a rushed interview, though he would miss Ty's lighting gear and expertise. If there was time, he could always rent equipment, and by then, Michaelyn would be along to help. He knew she was racing to meet him and had left a message at the hotel for her.

The car had a full tank of gas, and he would park as near as possible to the meeting. This time he would have his trusty backpack. He had plenty of charged batteries for cameras and his laptop. He even had a case of bottled water and an assortment of snacks and protein bars. If he did get surprised by something he wasn't prepared for, at least it would be a learning experience.

Ten minutes had now passed, and Jacob was considering shutting off the engine of the Hyundai, which had become toasty-warm inside. He had given up finding coverage or news of the event that was blocking traffic and had settled on an alternative rock station. The song had ended, and a disc jockey came on. "*Afternoon commuters look out for the Occupiers. They picked rush hour today to march from the university campus all the way to King Street to picket the financials. Outside of downtown, another clear and cool day, and nothing will stop you."* An advertisement started, and the cars in front of Jacob began to move forward at last, but slowly, as some drivers had shut off their engines, some had their cars out of gear, some were distracted, talking on the phone or reading newspapers. He didn't make it to the light in time and had to stop again as he watched Toronto Police Service officers eagerly getting back into their warm cruisers and out of the bitter cold.

CHAPTER TWENTY-FOUR

JULIE AND JACOB

Jacob froze, his Nikon strapped over his shoulder, and stared, his eyes widening in fright. Kitty-cornered from him was a black Chevy Caprice. He knew it was rare to non-existent, probably police-only specially made for export to Canada. The man inside it, dressed in black, had massive shoulders and a military haircut. Damn it! How long had this guy been on his tail? He should have known. Somebody was well aware of Jacob's movements. His instincts told him it was some sort of government surveillance, but he had no idea in reality. The man was looking right at him. He would have to get Julie away quickly.

Inside the Norwich Coffee Shop, Jacob stared at the front door, his feet doing a constant tap dance under the table, his fingers drumming on the tabletop. He sensed someone was watching him and looked at the barista station to see a lean, hawk-faced man, who quickly looked away, handing a cardboard-banded, snap-on-cap cup to a customer. Smiling slightly, the employee turned back to his machine, tapped espresso grounds out of the filter basket, and peered over the top. Jacob pulled out his Nikon for the third time and began polishing the lens, wondering if he was wearing out his welcome in the busy café.

It was 4:40 P.M. Jacob put away the Nikon and realized there was nothing on his table except an ad for a Jazz CD on a plastic stand. He supposed he should order something. The foot traffic in the shop was steady, but it was not crowded. He considered moving to the front of the shop but figured his spot near the back would provide more privacy for him and Julie when she arrived—*if* she arrived. He reckoned that if he were in her place, he might consider just picking up and leaving, even though she had really settled in here in Toronto. Nothing she would leave behind would be worth her life, which she might assume was in danger, depending on the circumstances of her disappearance ten years ago. Jacob felt exhilarated just being so close to finding out what those circumstances were but wary of the mystery man in the black car outside.

Julie walked in looking very serious but more confident and determined than when he had left her at midday. She carried her laptop case and wore a long navy overcoat. The sunny afternoon had faded into an overcast evening, and her coat was slightly damp with drops of rain or melted snow. She found him quickly. The shop was now emptying, though still busy, with most customers taking their orders out to meet a bus, taxi, or personal vehicle on the way home or elsewhere. Julie sat down without unbuttoning her coat, placing her laptop against the wall, and shoving her hands into her coat pockets. She glanced at him without meeting his eyes, not hiding anything. It was clear she was in a situation involuntarily, and he had put her there.

"We have to go. We're in danger." Jacob said, starting to get up.

Julie froze.

"I'm not going anywhere with you until I know what the hell's going on," she said.

"Okay," he said, the corners of his mouth tightening. "You want some coffee?" Jacob was trying to be patient. The meeting could have been a nice long listening session in which she told *him* what the hell was going on. But things had changed.

"Hot chocolate," Julie replied. He stepped up to the counter without waiting, ordered a regular brewed coffee for himself along with Julie's hot chocolate.

Liam took the opportunity to drop something in Jacob's coffee.

A distracted Jacob paid with a U.S. ten-dollar bill. He tried to remind himself that he was lucky Julie even showed up. When he got back to the table, she had removed her overcoat, revealing the double-breasted suit jacket that he had not seen at their earlier meeting. Her arms were folded on the table in front of her. As she removed the lid of her hot chocolate to take a scalding first sip, relishing the warmth of the cup and the steam coming from the top, she finally looked straight at him.

"The sheet in your folder said your name is Jacob?" She was not giving up anything before getting some answers from him.

"Yes," Jacob admitted. "I'm a videographer, mostly—a lot of still photography. I've worked on films and TV. News and documentary stuff."

"You said you were a journalist," Julie countered.

"That comes in when I have to go out and get my own story, which happens a lot," Jacob explained. Julie nodded. She didn't seem surprised. She could probably guess what kind of project he was working on. But her tone was very guarded. She was a long way from going anywhere alone with him.

"Why did you lie your way into my office?" she asked. On the outside, she wasn't softening a bit.

"Well," he began, "I didn't want to put you in the position of having to explain why a reporter was contacting you. And if I went up to you in the street or showed up at your home, well, I didn't expect you to be very receptive. At work, you can't make a scene, but you feel relatively safe," he said. "It was the best way I could come up with to contact you."

"Why should I trust you?" Julie knew she had to deal with Jacob one way or another. And she wanted to know how he had found her.

"I'm being pretty straightforward. And I've been seen in public with you, even though your receptionist didn't know my real name." Jacob knew no tricks when it came to this. He was just telling it like it was and hoping she would understand. If she didn't, he still had a story. Unfortunately, he might have to threaten her with going public regardless of whether she cooperated. "If I intended something sinister, I probably wouldn't have come to your office like that. You shouldn't be worried about me. Turn around and look outside. That's our problem right now."

CHAPTER TWENTY-FIVE

GOON

Julie laughed nervously and glanced around the coffee shop, her eyes briefly considering the shaggy-looking barista across from them. "Are you kidding?" she asked incredulously. Julie scanned the front windows.

"Across the street, there's a black car," Jacob said. "It's not a common one. Have you seen it before?"

"Never. So what?"

"I had a look at the guy driving it. He's definitely military or ex-military. He's just sitting there. I think he's been following one of us."

"Huh?" Julie froze.

"He might as well be wearing black fatigues and holding a sniper rifle," said Jacob. Julie read Jacob's face. She looked like she thought he had no idea what was going on. But she did not look threatened. Not by Jacob, anyway. "And that car he's driving is a police special: Corvette engine, the works. If you look closely, you can see the reinforced suspension underneath. And only sold in Canada."

"Look, as far as I know, he might be working with you," Julie said, staring off to her left. "So, what's your deal?"

"Huh?" His mind was racing now. His heart rate was up. They needed to move.

"You contacted me for some reason," said Julie. Her tone implied pity.

"Oh! Yes. I want to videotape an interview with you. We need to do it as soon as possible. Though, I'd like to bring some other people in if I can—a producer, technical people, an author I'm collaborating with." Julie just stared at him. "Of course," he continued, "you'll want some time to think about it. If you have any questions— listen, I'd love to talk more here, but we need to get away from that goon outside." Julie started shaking her head as soon as he started asking the question. She took a drink of her hot chocolate.

"Look, I'm no expert in these things by far," she said, "but the stuff you're interested in— whatever it is, and assuming you're telling the truth," she said, looking around, "there could be others if he's government or whatever. He was just the one you noticed." Jacob reminded himself to be patient. There was intrigue but not urgency in Julie's face. Why didn't she get it after what she's been through?

"Besides," she continued, "why would a guy like you describe be interested in me? I'm just a financial advisor. I don't even know anybody who's remotely as dangerous as what you're describing."

Jacob suddenly realized that someone might have brainwashed Julie. It made perfect sense, given the enormity of the secret she represented.

"You mean you don't know?" Jacob asked.

"Don't know what?" Julie replied, taking another drink of hot chocolate.

Before Jacob had time to answer, he felt his stomach tighten up, and a quickly-growing irritation in his bowels. "I'll be back," he said, and he ran toward the men's room.

CHAPTER TWENTY-SIX

BOLTED

When Jacob left for the bathroom, Liam saw his opportunity and seized it. He quickly poured the order he was working on and shoved it at the customer, grabbing a rag as he moved around the machines and partition that separated the baristas from the customers. As the operative made his way toward Julie's table, he wiped the empty table closest to him, moving the stand-up ad, straightening the chairs, and picking up a straw wrapper on the floor under the table. Then Liam moved to Julie's table, set his hand on it with the rag, leaned down, and looked her straight in the eyes. "Check out any CHARLIE CHAN movies lately?" he said, carefully and clearly, as Julie looked wide-eyed back at him. He continued past her, wiping tables quickly, moving around the room, staying out of Julie's way, but looking back at her every time he stopped at a table.

Julie looked around as if she didn't know why she was sitting there and had forgotten entirely about Jacob. Liam had removed Jacob's cup and everything else that was on the table. Julie stood and started putting on her coat. She finished her hot chocolate and left the cup on the table. Bending down to get her laptop, she slid her other hand into the pocket of her overcoat and turned to leave.

Emerging from the bathroom, Jacob said, "Oh, no!" into his phone. He had been trying to cryptically report to Josh as there was no time for an encoded message to him or Michaelyn. They had to lose this tail, and he needed some help.

"I gotta go!" he said and ended the call, shoving the phone into his pocket. Julie had disappeared quickly out the door almost before he knew it. Grabbing his backpack, he hurried to the door just in time to see a flap of her coat as she crossed the street. A bus was already there. He ran to the corner, but the light had changed, and the full brunt of rush-hour traffic swept away all hope of crossing the street in time. "Think!" Jacob said to himself.

He looked around. Well, at least he knew the goon was following him, not Julie. Bigger problem: Julie had bolted, and he had no idea where she was going. He noted the bus number, then ran to his car. Prioritize. Was she going home? He thought the conversation was going relatively well, considering the circumstances. Why would she show up and then leave without telling him?

Liam stared at the scene through the front window of the Norwich Coffee Shop, feeling the other barista glaring at him, who was now pulling all the shots. If the kid caught her, Liam might have more work to do. And in his experience, overtime is always dangerous. Maybe even deadly.

CHAPTER TWENTY-SEVEN

MADE

M3 sat in front of his laptop in the second-floor conference room. Another computer was on the other side, at the other end of the table. Elsewhere on the table, someone had stacked several folders and binders. The top one had the word "UNCLASSIFIED" stamped across it in big letters. Overhead were three rows of track lighting, two of them dimmed, the middle one off. Men and women in black suits and white French-cuffed shirts occasionally walked past outside the windows that lined two conference room walls.

M3 stared at the screen as he leaned his head on one fist, elbow on the table. As a weekend worker, he didn't have his own office. He shared one with his weekday counterparts, shift supervisors all. The problem was that all of them were usually there on Monday and Friday, so someone usually wound up in the conference room. As the last guy to show up, it was usually M3. Since he arrived late that morning, he had been to several meetings, all part of the inefficient but necessary turnover of information between shifts. Now he was just waiting for the weekday group to clear out so he could set up in his office for the weekend.

C3 walked into the room. He was in the same office-less predicament, with a slightly different meeting schedule, and his office had just become vacant. As he was gathering up his suit jacket, laptop, and files, he said, "Did you see the latest flash?"

M3 looked up from a long email he was composing.

"Huh?" He hated it when C3 caught him off guard.

"Your boy up north. Sideways. Good luck with that." C3 loved catching M3 off guard.

M3 looked down at the encrypted inter-office messaging program everyone kept running at all times. The heading was "Target J05248 made surveillance, in pursuit Chi recipient." He clicked on the title to see the whole message.

FROM: HF170
TO: C,H,M,FLASHUPDATE
RE: TARGET J05248
LOCATION: TORONTO
RELATED: CHI MESSAGE DELIVERED, INVOICE
FOR PAYMENT NSACA06399.

TARGET MADE SURVEILLANCE AFTER CONTACT
WITH M SYSTEM. SYSTEM PRESUMED ON
MISSION. TARGET IN PURSUIT. REPEAT
TARGET HAS NOT BROKEN OFF. CONTINUING
SURVEILLANCE PENDING FURTHER
INSTRUCTIONS.

He could tell without looking at the related message what had happened. And he knew what to do. As he got up, the laptop screen's motion sensor tripped the automatic locking feature, and the screen went black. "Faebaen?" he called out, skipping down the stairs to the C cubicles. A twenty-something man with jet black hair stood up to respond.

"She's in a meeting. I'm Darren. What do you need?"

"Darren. I remember you from a briefing a while back. Been here about a year?" M3 tended to focus intensely on one thing at a time. But he had a near-photographic recall, especially for faces and names.

"That's right, sir," said the young man. "Classified orientation overview of M Department. I'm impressed you remembered me. I finished my probationary period and just moved on to this shift as a staff analyst."

"Great. You should have no trouble with this. I need to open up a real-time voice line to a contract agent, 06399." M3 was comfortable with Faebaen, but he knew the C analysts were usually very dependable. Regardless of his tense relationship with C3, M3 knew the C department was solid in its selection and training process. In M3's area, skills were somewhat harder to quantify, and due to the esoteric nature of the work, personalities were often a problem. Not so with C Department. Their work was all technical, and you needed good technicians.

"I'm required to ask if it's possible to use text instead of voice," Darren said as they walked to the equipment cluster, "Since voice has less modulation, text is slightly more secure." Darren was very competent and absolutely by the book. On weekdays the message volume was much higher, and new techs got plenty of practice. And with the brass in the building, there was rarely a deviation from standard procedure. "And with voice, someone could overhear on the other end."

"Let's try text," said M3. "It's a negotiation, but I think we can do it with text." He watched as the new man entered codes into a computer encased in a kind of safe and applied a hardware key from his pocket. Darren requested biometric authentication, then they sat and waited for a response. M3 stood behind him. While they were waiting, Faebaen walked into the cubicle area, carrying a tablet computer.

"Are you getting everything you need, sir?" she asked him.

"Darren's got me all hooked up. Just waiting for a response. Have a good week?" M3 was usually all business, as was his nature, but he made a conscious effort to be personable and was successful at times.

"Good, thanks," Faebaen smiled. "When the authentication comes, you can take a seat and do the typing yourself if you want." Darren nodded his agreement.

Back in Toronto, Liam had hung up his apron, put on his coat, and was moving toward the door to walk into the dark, cold street outside. He felt a vibration at his ankle and reached down to draw the two-way pager out of its holster. Liam did this looking back to see if anyone was watching. Then he walked into a nearby alley, carefully checked both ends of it and overhead before reading his message.

M3: URGENT RT. PLEASE BM AUTHENTICATE

Liam started patting his pockets, looking for something. Finally, he withdrew from his inside coat pocket a two-inch by three-quarter-inch device that looked like a USB memory stick. He plugged it into the pager and waited for the screen to change. After a few seconds, the screen refreshed with the instructions, "Please scan your fingerprint to continue." He then pressed the middle finger of his right hand against the sensor on the USB device. The screen changed to "Your fingerprint was not recognized. Please try again." It was probably too cold. He pressed the enter button on the pager, breathed on the sensor and his finger, then pressed the sensor again. "Are you NSACA06399? Y or N?" He pressed enter a second time. Then he started the text exchange with NSA headquarters.

M3: EXTEND REQUEST MOST RECENT ASSIGNMENT WITH NEW INSTRUCTIONS. IDENTICAL TERMS.

M3 considered this question on the screen before him:

LIAM: HIGHEST LOI REQUESTED?

The agent wanted to know how close he had to get to the target, his level of interaction (LOI). The answer would tell him how potentially dangerous the mission was. Depending on the agent, he might request more money or turn down the assignment altogether. M3 wasn't familiar enough with this particular operative to know how comfortable he was with the business's physical side. The agent that had been "made" had military training and was expected to get physical at any time. This one was a relative unknown. Unfortunately, M3 didn't have much choice. His target was in a foreign country, so no resident agents were there. The system was on the move, so there was no time to send someone else. The only other alternative was to use CIA assets, and M3 knew that was almost certainly a career-ender, something he would never do unless under direct written orders. If he lied about the LOI, the agent could refuse to violate it later, so he was stuck. He sent the answer.

M3: DIRECT ACTION MAY BE REQUIRED.

LIAM: DOUBLE TERMS. TRIPLE IF DEADLY FORCE USED.

M3 nodded and pursed his lips. This operative was no idiot. He knew what they were asking him to do. They could tell him to take out the target completely, which would mean he could be on the run for a very long time, possibly the rest of his life. Thirty grand was a fair price if he had to take a murder rap. If it happened, the NSA would disavow him. M3 entered his response.

M3: DONE. ENGAGE TARGET AND PREVENT CONTACT WITH SYSTEM USING ANY AVAILABLE MEANS, CLANDESTINE IF POSSIBLE. DEADLY FORCE AUTHORIZED. IMPERATIVE TARGET NOT REACH CLEVELAND. REPORT HOURLY.

It was imperative that the system not be followed. It was even more important that no one tampered with it. High-functioning systems like this one had relatively light programming by necessity and were susceptible to deprogramming with little defense against a skilled deprogrammer. Even the untrained interloper could tip the delicate balance enough to interfere with the system's compliance with instructions. But at least now, they had someone on the job. Now, he had to talk to H3 about what had just happened and to arrange interception if the target was allowed to re-enter the U.S. He also needed them to tell the original surveillance agent to stand down; he was no good if the target knew him. He thanked the C techs and galloped back up the stairs.

CHAPTER TWENTY-EIGHT

LIAM

Liam ran across the street to catch the next bus. At this time of day, they were still running every ten minutes. He saw the bus two blocks up the street. He wasn't expecting this new assignment, so he didn't have the proper gear with him. It would be necessary to go either to his apartment or to a locker he kept at the ferry terminal. Since time was an issue, it might be better to go with the ferry terminal. But his apartment was relatively close to downtown, and there were more cars in the area, one of which he would need to steal. The bus arrived, and he stepped on, dropping a Loonie and a Toonie into the slot.

Several blocks later, he ran up the street and into his building. He said "hi" to the twenty-something blonde girl with the laptop bag who always seemed to pass him in the Lobby. The elevator was already going up, so he burst into the stairwell, taking stairs two at a time for a couple of flights. By then, he had had enough and trudged up the last two floors slowly, catching his breath.

Finally in his apartment, he quickly retrieved his laptop from the safe. Standing on his bed, he removed the ventilation grate and took out a .45 automatic pistol. He had never used the weapon and only bought it because he thought it looked cool in the movies. But now, he figured it might very well come in handy, as he was more likely to get into trouble than ever. Suddenly, this fact hit him, and he realized he had reached a kind of career milestone, or perhaps a life plateau. He wasn't sure if it was an achievement or a big step on the road to Hell. No time to think, though. He had a job to do, and it was a lot more demanding than pulling shots at Norwich.

The laptop finished booting, and a new message had come in. Due to time constraints, the agency bypassed the usual security protocols and sent data via encrypted email. The reason for the time-consuming and sometimes annoying procedures, such as getting faxes at several different copy shops, scanning, and decrypting on a special machine, was that encryption alone made the message public in encrypted form. It could be pulled out of the air by an enterprising hacker (even a poor one) with a standard protocol analyzer program. Once the hacker acquired the message, decryption began, and revealing the plain text was just a matter of time and processing power. The sender never wins and can only stay slightly ahead by having more powerful computers. That's why the NSA sent only the most time-sensitive messages this way.

In this case, Liam had inherited additional data about Julie that he had previously had no need to know. *Need to know* was a requirement for the dissemination of any classified information. Even someone with a Top Secret clearance could not access even Confidential-level information without a valid need to know such data. Julie's address was one such datum that would come in very handy at present. He jotted down the address. Then he put the laptop, pistol, and some other gear into a canvas bag and zipped it shut. A small case with specialized tools for breaking into and hot-wiring cars, he put in his coat pocket, and a slim-jim went inside his coat. Equipped and a little rested, he went out, locking the door behind him. The elevator was working. He found the lobby empty this time and rushed out the door, turning immediately to his left, where he knew there would be several cars on the street. He passed the blonde girl with the laptop bag he had seen earlier, now standing outside the door.

CHAPTER TWENTY-NINE

MICHAELYN

The clean-cut man sat in his car, waiting. He had been sitting there long enough that it was starting to get cold inside the car. He zipped up his leather jacket, then took a phone out of his inside jacket pocket. He took one last look ahead two blocks at Jacob's Hyundai, then started the car and moved out.

Jacob smiled as he watched the black Chevy Caprice drive away in his rearview mirror. He had taken down the license plate but couldn't do anything with it now. That kind of thing was handled by a specialist, private investigator, or hacker. The data was pseudo-public but not easily accessible. Julie seemed to think the guy had a military connection. Jacob had no idea who it might be. And for now, he was blissfully ignorant of anyone else that might be following him.

Jacob had parked his rental car outside Julie's apartment building. He'd lost contact with the bus but found her address through directory assistance. Fortunately, she had a landline in her apartment. He suspected that it might be one of those that came with the apartment. He wasn't sure what to do next. When he had seen her running across the street, she seemed different. Something about her face or the way she walked. He couldn't decide exactly what about her had changed. So far, he had not seen any sign of Julie here. He decided to call her.

"Hello?" she picked up on the first ring.

"Julie? It's Jacob."

"Who?" she sounded like she was busy, and he had interrupted something.

"Jacob, we just met today. We were talking at the coffee shop a while ago."

"Sorry, I don't know what you're talking about. I think you have the wrong number." She hung up. She hadn't confirmed who she was, but he recognized her voice. What could have happened to her in the few minutes he was in the bathroom? Jacob realized he was just going to have to wait there until she came out.

Around eight P.M, a text message came in:

I AM HERE M

Jacob thought about sending an encrypted message, but why bother? Whoever hired the guy in the Caprice knew where he was. He pressed the send button.

"Hello, this is Michaelyn."

"Hey, it's Jacob. Welcome to the team."

"Thank you. What's the story? They said you checked out." She sounded tired, but he knew she was excited to be involved in an investigation. She'd never done anything like this before.

"Yeah," said Jacob. "I'm on kind of a stakeout. It isn't part of the plan, just how things are working out. Why don't you check in, get some sleep, then meet me here in a few hours? If needed, you can take over, and I'll go sleep."

"Okay," said Michaelyn.

"I'll fill you in on what's going on when you get here. Otherwise, if anything happens, I'll call you." He knew they were already on somebody's radar, but there was no need to discuss anything unnecessarily over the phone.

"Sounds like a plan," she replied. "Can I ask one question, though? I didn't think to ask Ty about it, but is there, um, who's paying for all this? I mean, I want to help, I'm just wondering if there's some kind of—"

"Sure, sure. I think Josh has some funding already in place. But we need to pay upfront. Do you have a credit card you can use? Cash would be even better. If not, I can give you my info or something. He's pretty good about quick reimbursements, so you'll be able to pay your bill when it comes." Jacob scanned the street to make sure he wasn't distracted and missing something.

"No, I have cash," she said. "That's great. OK, I'll see you in a while."

"I'll text you the address," Jacob said. Just then, he saw Julie walk out of her building. "Uh...hey, Michaelyn, get here now. Yellowstone Street." He ended the call and got out of the car, walking toward Julie across the street. He called to her. She glanced back, then ignored him and walked faster around the corner and between two buildings. He walked a few steps more and looked at where she was going. There was a parking lot at the end of the alley. He got back in the car and started it up. He didn't know which way she was going, so he just drove around the block in the direction the car was pointed. A red Toyota left the parking lot coming straight toward him. As it passed, he saw clearly that Julie was the driver. "Oh-oh," he said to himself, hitting the gas and trying to make a u-turn in the narrow backstreet. At the same time, he tried to keep an eye on the red car to see which way Julie turned. She had already turned the first corner when he got turned and stomped on the gas. He skidded around the first corner, and she was already turning again. He floored it. Fortunately, she was turning right, and there were no other cars around. But the streets were slick from a light rain that was probably turning to black ice when it hit the roads. He felt the back end of the Hyundai slip a little as he made the second turn. Jacob silently vowed to be more careful. He'd be no good if he wrecked behind her. Of course, now he had Michaelyn as a backup.

They had entered the main thoroughfare, and Julie was two blocks ahead of him. He didn't know this area at all, but he recognized the street. He reached for his phone to call Michaelyn.

"I'm almost there!" said Michaelyn.

"We're on Finch now, going West, I think. Look, I'm pretty sure she's heading out of town. But I have no idea what direction." He was trying to catch up with Julie, who was now four blocks ahead.

"Wait a minute," Michaelyn said. "I'm looking at a map now. You're moving toward highway four hundred. That's how I came in. And I think I remember a Finch Street exit." Michaelyn was parked on the side of Yellowstone Street with her emergency lights on, reading the map with a flashlight in the old Mustang.

"It's coming up," said Jacob. "I say, go there. I'll let you know which way we go." Three blocks. "I'm on the move."

CHAPTER THIRTY

IMPACT

Jacob was staring ahead, trying to stay in visual contact with Julie's car, trying to keep track of where he was so he could relay the location back to Michaelyn, and trying to keep his car on the road as he sped up to keep Julie from getting away from him. He felt a strange quick rush of air and a squealing noise and took his eyes off the road to look in the direction of the noise. Then Jacob saw two headlights glaring at him through the rain-soaked driver-side window and heard the rapidly growing roar of a car engine. Suddenly, he saw nothing but white all around him, and he heard nothing but the sound of metal creaking and plastic crunching.

A sharp pain stung his side, and his wrists and face burned. Jacob opened his eyes to the deflating white airbag. He smelled baby powder, and dust floated in the air around him. Cold air was coming in from the left side—not just the window, but the entire left side. A black Honda Civic was pointed straight at Jacob's car, its front bumper embedded in his left door. A skinny young man with 1970's-style hair and a backpack had just managed to pry the Honda's door open and was stepping out. Jacob just stared, dazed. The man finally got his long leg out of the car. He took a long look at Jacob, then looked down the road toward where Julie must be. Then he turned around and started running down the side street he had come from.

Suddenly Jacob realized he wasn't breathing. He gasped several times, involuntarily gulping air until his lungs opened up, and he could breathe normally again. The accident had knocked the wind completely out of him. Somewhere in the car, he heard a high-pitched voice calling his name.

"Jacob!" He groaned, feeling the pain in his side as he leaned to his right to grab his phone.

"Michaelyn. I had a wreck. If you're coming up Finch, don't stop. Do you understand?"

"Jacob. Are you okay? Why don't you want me to stop?" she sounded incredulous.

"Somebody's watching me," he said. "Head for the highway and go south. You're looking for a red Toyota, license plate '999-SLJ'." A pale-faced woman in a black jacket was walking up to the car. A few wisps of blonde hair peeked from under her black knit cap.

"He's alive," she said into a radio. "Get EMS."

He smiled at her, almost drunk, as he crashed from the adrenaline surge of the last few minutes. "I gotta go," he said into the phone.

"Is anybody there?" Michaelyn was coming up Finch and saw what must be an unmarked police car. A red light was flashing from inside the car. She pressed the END button and stomped on the gas pedal as she passed them. This whole job was up to her now, and she wasn't going to let Jacob down. She looked way down the road ahead of her. There was only one car turning in from a side road. She blew right through the red light at the Highway and barreled toward the onramp, trying to ease the wheel left without skidding. The Mustang rolled heavily, and she heard the suspension creak at the apex of the turn. Then she slapped the shifter, downshifting to second gear and easing into the gas. As she merged onto the highway, there was more traffic than there was on Finch, but only a few vehicles were in sight. None of them were red. She grabbed third gear and kept the pedal down.

CHAPTER THIRTY-ONE

ELLIE

"Where are you hurt?" The girl in the black coat asked Jacob.

"Left side, ribs," he replied. "I think everything else is good." He was sore but not in constant pain. He must have been knocked out for a second but was lucid enough now to regret losing Julie. The blonde was speaking to him again.

"You might have a concussion. Better stay put until the paramedics arrive." She looked to her left and made a circular motion with her hand in the air.

"Are you a cop?" Jacob asked, dazed.

"CSIS. Kind of like your CIA, FBI, and Secret Service all put together." She had stowed her radio and shoved her hands into her pockets.

"Oh yeah, I'm American," he smiled. The girl nodded. She knew. "My name's Jacob." He stuck out his right hand.

"Ellie." She shook his hand.

Jacob withdrew his hand to rest on the seat beside him. Then he started to raise his left arm to the window and noticed it was covered in blood. "Oh." More flashing lights appeared around him, and Ellie motioned to the ambulance that had just arrived.

Minutes later, he sat on a gurney inside the ambulance. The paramedic was finishing applying a bandage to his left arm. Ellie had taken some information on a clipboard and was handing it to a TPS Officer. She walked back over to him as he was stepping out of the ambulance.

"They let you go?" she said.

"Ribs are just bruised, and some cuts on my arm." Jacob looked around for his stuff. "I guess I need a cab." He reached into a pocket for his phone.

"Why don't I give you a ride," said Ellie. She picked up one of his bags and started walking back to the unmarked car with the flashing red light.

Driving back down Finch, Ellie and Jacob sat side by side in the government sedan's front seat. "So," said Jacob, "You like being a spy?"

"Some times more than others," Ellie said, glancing over at him with a quick smile. "That guy could have been trying to kill you, you know."

"You saw him?" Jacob thought the guy just panicked and ran away. "Why do you think he was trying to kill me?"

"He ran into you on purpose. I was hoping you could tell *me* why." Ellie took off her cap as the car warmed up and let her hair fall loose around her shoulders. Jacob felt a bit dazed. Maybe the paramedic had given him something for pain.

"He must be stupid or crazy," Jacob said. "I saw him, and there's the license plate. Probably a registration in the car. What made him think he could get away with it?" Ellie's instincts told her Jacob knew more than he was saying. It was the classic ruse of talking a lot but not saying anything.

"The car was stolen," said Ellie. "That's why we were following him. We hoped he would lead us to a chop shop that's part of a national auto theft ring. But he had other plans." Ellie was also playing her cards close. "So, what do you do?"

She had seen his camera equipment. He was traveling light. "Photographer," answered Jacob. "I'm just on vacation, though."

"Looks like you brought your work with you." They were approaching the airport. Up ahead were overhead arrival and departure signs. "I noticed your camera bag."

"No, I mean, it's not just a job for me. I love it. I'm never without a camera." Jacob took the opportunity to not-so-subtly size up Ellie's form. "You know, you could be a model. You have the presence."

Damn right, she could. "Get right out of town!" she said, grinning as she turned on the emergency flashers.

"No, I'm serious. You definitely have some talent. I could put together a portfolio for you." More distraction and misdirection.

"I don't know about that, but here's my card," Ellie said. "Give me a call if you think of why Honda boy might have been after you." She flashed a smile at him once more, closing the trunk as he removed his bags. "Good luck with the rental company." Jacob watched as she got in the car and drove away. Then he looked at her card and smiled. His phone rang.

CHAPTER THIRTY-TWO

LAKE ONTARIO

"Hello?" Jacob tried to gather his bags with one hand while holding the phone. That wasn't going to work. He started putting on the backpack.

"What happened? Are you okay?"

"Michaelyn. Yes. Uh, did you—?" He was now walking toward the terminal doors.

"Yes," said Michaelyn. "I'm still following her, and I have to pee like a friggin' racehorse!" She sounded frustrated and focused, and Jacob's focus had slipped away. He had to clear his head. He looked at his watch. An hour had passed.

"Don't worry, she's human too. Look, I'm banged up but still on duty. Just stay with her. Where are you now?" He walked toward the rental car counter.

"We're approaching the border," she said. "Looks like she's headed for the good ole U.S.A."

"And you didn't even stay long enough to get a postcard," Jacob quipped. "Look, I gotta take care of some business. Call me back in an hour or if something changes."

"Okay, Jake. I'm glad you're still in one piece," Michaelyn said, hanging up. Jacob looked at the night clerk at the rental counter and smiled.

"It's okay," the clerk said. "The cops called and said they saw the guy hit you. Our insurance company will call you to get a statement, but I can give you another car now if you need one."

Jacob looked surprised and pleased. "Well, well, well," he said in his smoothest voice. "You Canadians are so nice. Yes, please, I would like a car. Something with a little zip this time."

Half an hour later, he was on the ferry, looking over the side at the water splashing down the side as the craft cut through Lake Ontario at full speed. He finished off a Rock Star energy drink, tossed it in a trash bin, and opened the door of his new rental, a maroon Hyundai, just like the one the guy in the stolen Honda had just destroyed, with no more zip. He plugged his phone into the accessory jack on the console, then speed-dialed Josh.

"Jake. This is not a secure line." Josh was awake and alert and still vigilant about keeping their secret.

"They know we're on to Julie," said Jacob. "I had no idea, but Julie knew. But they don't know how much we know or what the status is now. Unless they were listening to my cell phone for the past couple hours."

"Who's 'they'?" Josh knew it could be law enforcement, intelligence arms from any of several governments, other media, someone protecting Julie, some unknown criminal element, or something completely different.

"I don't know," replied Jacob. "I think Julie knows, but I didn't get enough time with her to find out. One of the guys was being watched by Canadian Intelligence, though. The one that rammed my rental car with me in it." Jacob winced as he tried to work out some soreness by rotating his left arm.

"Wow, are you okay?" Josh asked. "What about Michaelyn?"

"Both fine. I'm on a ferry headed back into New York. Michaelyn is, uh, otherwise occupied." Jacob knew they still had to be careful.

"Send me a message if you have time. You need anything?" Josh was eager to do anything. He was getting restless sitting in the Seuss Motel waiting.

"Josh, there's a problem," Jacob began. "Julie split on me right in the middle of a conversation, and the last time I saw her, she didn't know me, even though I had been talking with her face-to-face an hour or so earlier." Jacob stared out the window at the clouds overhead, threatening snow, sleet, or rain. "I'm not sure what to do."

"You're sure it was her, and she wasn't just acting like she didn't know you—you know, because someone was watching?" Josh asked.

"I'd swear she thought she didn't know me," Jacob replied. "And I've studied her enough to know if it was someone else, even someone trying to look like her. It's like a switch was flipped."

"I'm trying to think if we know any psychiatrists or anybody like that. Because the only other option is that her mind is messed up, or she's drugged or something," said Josh.

"She seemed lucid enough when she sped away in the car, but almost like a different person." Jacob let his head tilt back on the headrest and closed his eyes. "I do know one doctor that might help us. And I'm pretty sure his number is still in my phone." After his father died, Jacob had seen a psychiatrist for a few months, and on and off since then. But it had been a couple of years since they had spoken.

"You give him a call then. Listen, Jake," Josh commanded, "Don't hesitate. I think we need to act now and not just follow her until she falls into the wrong hands. Don't break any laws, but find a way to get to her and take her off the market. Understand?"

"Yeah, I'm on it," Jacob said. "Stand by for a message." They hung up. Jacob took the rest of the time on the ferry to send a coded update on where Michaelyn and Julie were. His next call was to his old therapist, Dr. Green.

CHAPTER THIRTY-THREE

OPERATIONS CENTER

M sat in an oversized leather chair on an elevated platform at the back of the large room known as the Operations Center. He wore a dark grey V-neck sweater over a button-down grey shirt with no tie. His pale face had decades of concern carved into its corners, hills, pools, and valleys. Slowly thinning hair obediently streamed from an indeterminate point on his scalp straight back in patches of dark grey, silver, and white. His legs were crossed, and he held a pair of horn-rimmed half-focal reading glasses in one hand. His appearance reflected not just the experience required of a senior executive but many additional years of study and expertise in a discrete scientific endeavor. He was a professor, a lion, a living intellectual ancestor.

M endlessly doted on his creations, wherever they were, for their entire lives. He cared not that it was approaching midnight. He felt like a father called in to care for a sick child. The careerism of his underlings was a constant irritation to him. They had not yet reached the maturity level when one realizes the insignificance of such things. It was the work. The work was the only thing that mattered. It required constant attention. It required love, cruelty, joy, horror, abuse. All of these were tools of his trade, and he and his subordinates needed to apply them with conscientious precision. M3 was one of his best managers, but that's all he was. M wanted disciples, "fishers of men." But in the context of NSA bureaucracy, save a chance miracle in the screening and hiring process, managers were about all he could hope for. Elsewhere, he could find disciples. But it wasn't safe out there.

M3 was pacing, looking over the shoulders of technicians all over the room. The Operations Center was a place where a number of humans and machines met together to build an overall picture of a particular agency operation or mission. Representatives from H (Human Intelligence), C (Communications), S (Signals, Space, and Satellites), and I (Cyber Intelligence) had permanent workstations. Other areas were brought in as suited the needs of the particular mission. M Department had a records librarian with access to all of the historical data on the subject system, including video, audio, medical records, and all surveillance and tracking logs. Two technicians were on hand this evening, searching through years of information for bits to help locate Julie and protect the information she represented.

M3 had called in M due to the complication of Jacob identifying the field operative that was tailing him. Normally, this might not have concerned the department head after hours on a Friday, but Julie represented a unique set of information, and her situation was fragile. M3 had been proud that his decision to put the inexperienced Liam on a direct-action mission had worked out. Jacob had been effectively knocked off the trail without the massive attention that a murder would attract. They were still in the dark about Julie, but at least no one else was on to her, and she was presumably on her way in.

"You should have involved me earlier in this," M said, disappointment dripping from his lips.

"I didn't want to bother you, sir," M3 replied. M knew this reluctance was a failing not only of his subordinate but of himself in not properly training an off-shift manager.

"It's Big Wedding, damn it," M snapped. "Have I ever chastised you for getting me out of bed for anything?" M3 nodded, not in response but in the understanding of his mistake. "Do we have tracking on the girl?" M asked no one in particular. All departments were at his command for this mission. He answered only to the Deputy Director.

The S tech answered. "No radio or RF tracking available on the vehicle. Ten minutes to satellite acquisition. All drones in the region are either down or on deployment, sir."

"What about other military surveillance?" M wondered why they had only used drones when legacy reconnaissance aircraft were available.

M3 answered. "Not viable due to classification of the system, sir. None of our own air units are within range, so I didn't want to take the chance of this leaking out through the Air Force."

"Better than leaking out through CNN! We can wait for satellite, though, I suppose." M wasn't here to run things. He was as hands-off as any department head when it came to field operations. But he wasn't above imparting some of his vast institutional wisdom when he saw fit to do so.

"Got her!" said one of the technicians. S Section had border-patrol video. M3 walked to the tech's station and looked over her white-shirted shoulder. "She entered the U.S. at Rochester, New York, around 2145."

"Good," said M3. At least, she was heading in the right direction. He walked over to H section's console. "We need to get a man on the girl. And what about our contract agent in Toronto?"

"He's hot, sir. He's been made by the target, and local police have him on their wanted list for auto theft and a hit and run," the H tech said, scanning through police reports and writing up a status log. "No way he'd make it across the border." M3 thought about the twenty grand he was going to see in the budget report next week.

"Closest asset inside the U.S. is embedded Civil Air Patrol, Stratton, New York," said the H tech.

"Put him in a car instead of a plane, so he can go on foot if necessary," M3 barked.

"Sending to your screen," the H tech replied, looking over at C Section. On his screen was a standard message template customized for the asset.

"Got it," said the C tech. He looked back at the S Section. "Send me the latest long and lat on the system."

"Done," said the S tech. "You've got lat and long on the border crossing at Rochester, but fresh Satellite video is coming in. You can wait, or we can send an update in five."

"Initial activation sent," said the C tech. "Requested immediate status report."

"Satellite video has her at Buffalo heading west." S Section. "Lat and long on your screen, C."

"Asset is en route and will intercept, was already in his vehicle," H Section reported.

"Updated system location sent," said the C tech.

"Good work," said M3. "Now, don't lose her. Surround her with love, and don't let anyone near her."

"Bring me the system file," said M. One of the M techs handed him a tablet PC showing a picture of Julie and a short biography. He began to flip through the pages of the file. There were some pornographic images and videos, a list that had code words in one column and Greek letters in another. There was a page with two hand-drawn pictures. They both resembled Julie. Next to each was the word "Alter," followed by a name. Below this was another brief bio and other attributes such as "Age" and "Role." M called for M3 to come over. "You know the system is quite fragile. We programmed her to be high-functioning in the real world. The split is subtle."

"A dual system. I'm familiar with them." M3 had not studied Julie's file in depth, but he knew the category of system he was dealing with and the basic features.

"What this means is..." M pointed a finger at the file for emphasis. "An untrained person could flip her if that person is persistent enough." He spoke very slowly. "We can't allow that to happen. If there is any possibility, the system must be destroyed. Do you understand?"

"Yes, Sir. We have assets moving into position that will ensure this." M3 looked at M with as serious a look as he could manage. M appeared to be satisfied, though still annoyed. He leaned back in his chair again, handing the tablet to M3.

CHAPTER THIRTY-FOUR

INTERVENTION

"You have to grab her," Jacob said. They were still speeding down the interstate.

"What!" Michaelyn suddenly wished she was back on her ratty old couch in Boston with a big bowl of buttery popcorn, watching a video with Steve, or doing some other equally uneventful thing. She had never thought she would be doing anything other than getting coffee, swapping camera batteries, or maybe operating a video camera if she was lucky. But ever since she arrived in Toronto, she'd felt more like an FBI agent than a film intern on a documentary.

"Next time she stops, you need to confront her and get her to cooperate," Jacob explained. "Josh thinks she's headed to a place where she may disappear, and we'll never see her again.

And I've already had two goons on my tail. They may have American brothers."

"How in the Good Christ—excuse me, Jake— am I going to do that?" Michaelyn thought Jacob was out of his mind. She didn't have a clue how to do this, and she was scared.

"I have some help for you. I'm still coming, by the way. I'm almost to Buffalo."

"You'll never catch us," Michaelyn said. "She's been going almost eighty all the way. I almost lost her when we stopped for gas. I think you're wrong. She's not human." She felt better talking with Jacob like this but still did not see any way she could "grab" Julie.

"An old friend of mine will be calling you in a few minutes," offered Jacob. "He's a psychiatrist. I'll text you his number so you can call him if you need to."

"Jake, what am I going to say? What would you say?" Michaelyn was slowly coming around to the possibility that she would confront Julie. But she doubted that Jacob knew any more than she did about how to handle this.

"Man, I'm sorry you're in this position. I'd rather it was me. But you can do this."

"First, tell her you're a friend of mine," Jacob instructed. "Remind her of everything that happened today. Deep down, she knows I'm her friend, and she should see you in the same light. Tell her that we need her cooperation. Until her story is public, she will always be in danger from someone trying to silence it. Tell her it's important. She's our only link to what really happened on 9/11. Then just hope and pray. She's either been drugged or hypnotized or something, so we're just taking the best stab at this we can."

"If it's the only way, I'll give it a try. Who knows, maybe it will work." She gave her Mustang the gas to keep from falling farther behind. "Anything else?" she asked.

"I'm not giving up. I'm still back here. Let's hang up. Julius will be calling soon. Good luck." Before Michaelyn could get her thanks out, they hung up.

Michaelyn did indeed hear from Jake's psychiatrist friend, Julius, who gave her some general advice on how to appear non-threatening to Julie, which would be the most crucial part of any interaction. If Julie were afraid, which she naturally would be, not only would she not listen, she would probably move away as quickly as possible.

Michaelyn went through the words she would say in her head, trying not to feel the anxiety of the moment every time she went through them. But she was very nervous despite the advice, despite the instructions, and despite Jake's reassurances. She didn't think she would be hurt, at least not by anyone she knew was involved at this point. Her worst fear was of failure, not turning Julie around, and scaring her off so that they would never be able to get her story.

Up ahead, she saw a blinker on the Toyota come on. A sign for an upcoming rest area had just passed on the right. "Thank God!" Michaelyn whispered. Julie Foley was human, after all. Michaelyn floored it. It was time. She hoped it would all be over quickly, one way or another. It had been a very long day, but she felt the adrenaline pumping through her wrists as she gripped the wheel, through her legs as she worked the pedals, and into her heart, now pounding harder than she thought it could.

The flat blue of the Mustang's hood came into view under the street lamps as the exit ramp became a curved, narrow road that ran between the sparse trees and grassy sections of the park-like roadside retreat. Posts as big as small tree stumps connected by chains lined the road on both sides. There were no other cars parked there. In a distant parking lot, several over-the-road trucks were parked for the night.

The red Toyota sat empty in a straight parking spot on the right side of the lot. It would allow Julie to get in and out faster. To the left were some slanted spots, closer to the main building containing the restrooms, snack machines, and wall-mounted maps of the area.

As Michaelyn rolled past the Toyota to back the Mustang into the parking space in front of Julie's car, she noticed that the rain had stopped long enough for most of the road and concrete walks to be dry now. Michaelyn could not hear the wind from inside the Mustang. As she took her foot off the pedals and let go of the wheel, she relaxed a bit, but she set her jaw and fixed her eyes on the Toyota in her rearview mirror. Julie would be in the restroom. Michaelyn would have to meet her at the car and prevent her from entering it. She cracked her window to hear, as well as see, what was happening in the rest area around her. Don't be threatening, she reminded herself, but contain her initially, long enough to get the message out.

As she got her jacket on inside the Mustang, she heard a door and looked over at the building. There was a brightly lit passageway between the car and truck parking areas. No one was there. Michaelyn breathed out. Just then, the door opened to one of the restrooms, hinged away from her so she couldn't see who was coming out until the door started closing. She tensed up again. A middle-aged man emerged with a ball cap over white hair, suspenders over a chambray shirt, and jeans. He strolled toward the truck lot, stretching his arms and twisting his torso, probably on a brief stop or just waking up from a sleep break.

Michaelyn made sure the driver's side door to the Mustang was unlocked. Engine off, she put her keys in her pocket, zipped up her jacket, and turned her legs so she could jump out quickly without hitting the steering wheel. Hand gripping the door handle, she sat coiled. She didn't want Julie to see her before she got close to the car. Waiting is hell on earth, she thought. "Come on!" Michaelyn whispered to herself. Now that she was ready, she had had enough suspense.

Julie walked out of the restroom, bought a bottle of iced tea from a vending machine, and walked briskly toward the car. She glanced at the Mustang, but Michaelyn had ducked low enough that Julie wouldn't see her. Waiting until Julie was a few feet from the Toyota, she pulled the door handle so hard it almost came off in her hand. Julie quickly looked at the figure springing from the car. She hesitated for a moment as it might just be another traveler stopping for a break. When she saw Michaelyn was headed straight for her, she lunged for the car, but Michaelyn swiftly cut her off. "Please listen to me for just a second," said Michaelyn, holding both hands up in a "stop" gesture.

"I'm in a hurry. Please get away from my car," Julie said sternly.

"I want to help you. I'm with Jacob. Do you remember talking with Jacob in the coffee shop today?" Michaelyn held her ground, trying to connect with something, anything. Julie wrinkled her brow.

"No. And if you don't move, I'm calling the police." Julie's words were harsh, but she was apprehensive, glancing around for any accomplices. Michaelyn could identify with Julie's predicament and thought she might have been looking for stronger, more dangerous accomplices. Julie took her phone out of her coat pocket.

"I don't think you want to call the police, Julie. You are in trouble, and this is very important." Michaelyn was gambling. If the tables were turned, she would have probably called the police. Julie did not move to dial her phone, apparently feeling less physically threatened but still uneasy and troubled.

"Who are you? How do you know my name?" Michaelyn was connecting with the deep-down personality Jacob had talked about. Something in the back of Julie's mind was telling her to listen, as long as it was safe. They could see headlights approaching. Slowly a large SUV came into view. They could see two men inside.

"We don't want to be standing out here," Michaelyn warned her. Julie's eyes registered agreement. "Give me your keys. We'll get in the car and talk." Julie hesitated, giving her a sideways look of doubt. "I know you want to trust me. Let me say what I have to say. Then you can decide what to do."

"I'll keep the keys," said Julie. "But you can sit in the driver's seat. Deal?"

"Okay," said Michaelyn, relieved. Julie pressed the unlock button on her remote and walked around to the other side of the Toyota. They both quickly got in and locked the doors.

As they sat side by side in the front seats, Julie, still wary, did not take her eyes off this new intruder in her life. Michaelyn looked straight ahead, breathing, trying to relax and gather her thoughts. "Do you remember anything about today?" she started. Julius had mentioned that Julie might have been given a drug to affect her memory. This possibility made sense, as she had run away after meeting Jacob in a coffee shop. It would have been easy for someone to put something in the coffee.

Julie was still staring at Michaelyn. "I want some answers before I answer anything. Who are you?"

"Okay," Michaelyn agreed, "But please keep in mind that someone has been following Jacob, and they are probably looking for you right now." She told Julie everything that she knew, repeating what Jacob had told her about his two meetings with Julie that day. Whenever Michaelyn mentioned Jacob's name, Julie's face changed.

"So, all of this is about a stupid movie?" Julie was relieved and upset at the same time. "I've been asleep, so I don't remember anything about today. And I need to get back on the road. Your movie can wait."

"So, where are you going in such a hurry? And why is it so important that you get there?" Michaelyn was growing more confident.

"I'm going to Cleveland," said Julie. Suddenly she looked confused and stared ahead as if she was trying to remember why she was driving to Cleveland. Then she shook her head. "I ... don't know why, exactly. But I'm sure it's something important."

"Listen to what you're saying. You don't remember what happened today. You don't remember why you're going to Cleveland." Michaelyn started to feel sorry for Julie, who was looking more and more confused and discouraged. "I think you need someone to trust right now. You trusted Jacob."

"Jacob?" Julie was starting to cry and was no longer staring down Michaelyn. She looked at the floor as Michaelyn continued.

"Yes, Jacob," said Michaelyn. "He's a good person. So am I. We can help you." Now, Julie was becoming more energetic and desperate.

She looked around the car, then straight at Michaelyn.

"Jacob." Julie was only speaking in syllables now. Michaelyn was starting to get uneasy. "Help me."

For a moment, the only sound was the wind and the slamming doors of the SUV, which had parked in one of the slanted parking places. Two teenage girls were piling into its back seat and slamming their doors as well. Julie sniffed, tears flowing down her face.

"Jacob!" she shouted, looking Michaelyn in the eyes, searching for help there. "Take me! Please take me." The look was a longing one, full of desperation and desire. Julie had not touched Michaelyn, but all the same, Michaelyn felt suddenly crowded and unable to deal with this situation.

"Just relax, Julie," Michaelyn said, holding up a hand as if to place a reassuring hand on the weeping woman's shoulder but not wanting to touch her. "Stay here with the doors locked. Don't go anywhere. I'm going to go make a phone call." Maybe Julius had a solution for this. "Okay?" Julie was dazed, or in a trance, and just sat still quietly, whispering Jacob's name and the words "Take me." When she turned and looked forward again, Michaelyn felt confident enough that Julie wouldn't try to run away and quietly got out of the car to stand in the once-again-empty parking lot.

Remembering Josh's cautioning instructions, which she had written down earlier that day when on the phone with him, Michaelyn made straight for the payphone between the restrooms. Now that she was in contact with Julie, she thought it would be safer than her cell phone, and she needed to put a little distance between herself and Julie. From the parking lot, the building was slightly downhill. It seemed colder here than it had been north of the border, she thought. Pulling out a credit card, she dialed the psychiatrist's number.

CHAPTER THIRTY-FIVE

DIAGNOSIS

Julius Chrysostom Green sat in a brown leather wingback chair with legs crossed. He was half-watching a comedy show on television and half-reading the *New England Journal of Medicine*. His wife sat next to him, doing the same with her knitting. Julius was a distinguished-looking African-American man in his fifties. From time to time, he chuckled, either at the television show or at whatever he was reading in the journal. He wore reading glasses and a cardigan sweater that was several shades of brown and knitted by Mrs. Green. It went nicely with his chair. As the phone rang, he stood up to walk to his home study, where he had a separate line. It was common for him to get calls from patients at all hours, a sacrifice that Mrs. Green had grown to understand, though she still did not prefer it.

The study was small. Not large enough to see patients in, although he had met them here, and just about everywhere else in the greater New York area during his long career. It was stocked with many generally older books. He kept the latest material at his office. He didn't spend a lot of time in the study, but it was convenient, especially when he was working on writing an article or that book he kept piddling at. It had a window on one wall with wooden blinds that he always kept open. There was no computer, though he had a laptop in a bag somewhere. There were no filing cabinets and no papers on his desk. He liked it uncluttered and thought this helped him to think more clearly. The clutter belonged at the office.

Julius had spoken to Michaelyn earlier and was not surprised to hear from her again.

"I've contacted her," Michaelyn began, "and things were going well until suddenly she started getting scared and really..." She paused as if she didn't want to say what she needed to tell him.

"Just relax, child. Whatever it is, just tell me as best you can." Julius spoke as if nothing was new under the sun for him.

"Well, it just seemed like she was coming on to me. Though she kept saying Jacob's name."

"She said Jacob's name every time?" Julius asked. Wheels were turning in his head. His mind scanned thirty years of cases, studies, and training in a microsecond for the appropriate information and questions needed to narrow down the diagnosis. "And you're sure it was a sexual advance?"

"Absolutely," Michaelyn replied. "She didn't touch me, but I could see it in her eyes. It seemed like someone else was speaking."

Julius had a possible diagnosis.

"I still don't have enough information," Julius said. "I would need to examine her, of course. But this could be a case of mind control programming via trauma, resulting in Dissociative Identity Disorder, or DID, also known as Multiple Personality Disorder." He turned on a desk lamp and leaned back in his high-backed chair.

"You mean schizophrenia?" asked Michaelyn.

"In popular jargon, yes. But that term refers to a completely different disease. Julie may have two distinct personalities or *alters*. One of them is the one Jacob met in Toronto. The other just came to prominence in her, perhaps for the first time in years, when you confronted her. Now, the system connecting and controlling the two may be breaking down."

"What does that mean, Doctor Green?" asked Michaelyn.

"It means we have an opportunity to help her. You see, DID can theoretically be an adverse effect of therapy but is also known to be caused by childhood trauma. She may see you, or Jacob, as her new controller and may be asking you, through the sexual advance, to reprogram her." The doctor was already glancing around his study for some reference material, now wishing he had a cordless phone there. He couldn't reach the light switch or see the bookshelves on the far wall of the study.

Michaelyn groaned. "Wow. I hope you're not saying I have to do this reprogramming or whatever."

"She's seriously ill, Michaelyn. She needs to be under a doctor's care. But the good news is she's receptive. So you should be able to transport her—to me, if possible."

"Hmmm. Okay," said Michaelyn. "That's good news and another challenge. Thanks, Julius." She sounded exhausted by everything she'd had to deal with that day.

"One more thing," said Julius. "It's also possible that someone inflicted the trauma precisely to cause the split of her personality. In that case, someone else has an interest in her, and they may be looking for her now."

"I haven't seen anyone so far, but Jacob's been followed, so maybe it's the same people. Thanks for the warning. I probably need to get back to her, and I need to call Jacob."

"Well, good luck," offered Julius. "I'm here if you need me." They said goodbye and hung up. Julius turned on the light and found a volume on hypnosis in ancient Egypt. This was not satisfactory. He needed to go to his office. Mrs. Green would not be pleased.

Michaelyn had been warily watching to make sure Julie stayed put. She now looked across the compound at her charge, who had fallen asleep. She checked the map on the front of the building, pulling her cell phone from the front pocket of her jeans. She selected Jacob and hit the 'Send' button.

"I think we can move her," reported Michaelyn. "Julius wants us to bring her to him."

"Too far, too risky, not enough time. I'm approaching a rest stop, and this one might be yours. We need to find a safe house nearby."

"But he said she's very sick. She needs a doctor." Michaelyn was conflicted now. Although she was sure that they were taking Julie away from a bad situation, she was worried that they couldn't give her the medical attention she needed.

"We'll just have to work with Julius over the phone. Look, she's in danger now. She, uh,

I think I just found you. I'm pulling up behind Julie's car." Michaelyn could see him now and hung up the phone. Jacob got out and walked toward the building.

"Good work," he said, smiling slightly. "We gotta figure out what to do with these cars."

"Yeah, we can't let her drive." Michaelyn crossed her arms, feeling sorry for Julie.

"There's a quiet little hotel in Lakeview, just across the Pennsylvania border. I stayed there once on a cross-country drive. I'm looking up the nearest place I can return this rental." Jacob feverishly tapped on his smartphone.

"Shouldn't we turn back east now?" asked Michaelyn. It was a logical idea, though, in her mind, she still wanted to get home. At some point, they would all have to sleep.

"Okay, we're going to a rental place in the next town, just a few miles away. But first, I need to send a coded message to Josh, so people can meet us, um..." They both looked at the wall-mounted map. Jacob raised his left arm to trace their path along I-90, but flinched and quickly lowered it.

"Ouch. Did the paramedics give you anything for pain?" Michaelyn had noticed his discomfort.

"Yeah, but I had to dump them at the border."

"You got searched?" she had never heard of anyone being searched at the Canadian border. Mexican, yes, but not Canadian.

"I always get searched, Michaelyn," Jacob said wearily. "You get involved enough in what we do, and they'll start searching you every time too. It's part of the job." He was starting to look normal again. "I couldn't drive with those pills anyway. I'll get something at the hotel. What do you think?" He nodded at the map.

"We could go south," Michaelyn replied, "but I say we go all the way to Buffalo. It will have whatever we need, maybe even a doctor we can trust, and it's only a few hours for the reinforcements. If we keep going south, they'll never get to us through those mountains, at least not without getting lost. Plus, turns out Julie was headed for Cleveland. I'm thinking we don't want to meet whoever's waiting for her there."

"Okay," agreed Jacob. "I need to send Josh an encrypted message first. We'll update him with where we're staying once we get there. Go ahead and update Julie if she's awake. And move her to the rental with me and anything she brought with her. Hopefully, she remembers me now and will be more comfortable that way."

"And I'll feel a lot better about it. This has been a crazy experience, Jacob. But I feel like I have been a part of something important."

Jacob smiled and nodded. Michaelyn swelled at this small sign of approval.

"Be ready to follow me in your car. We'll leave hers here. I'll pull out as soon as I get the message sent." Michaelyn nodded. They took turns using the restroom, one of them always watching Julie, still motionless in the Toyota, which would soon be cool enough inside to wake her.

As Jacob finished sending his message, Julie sat down in the passenger seat of his rental car, shivering. She still looked scared. But she gave Jacob a look that assured him that her trust was focused on him, and her fear was focused outside the vehicle.

"We'll be leaving soon. We're going someplace where you'll be safe," Jacob reassured Julie. "Are you cold? I'll get some heat going." Julie nodded and took a drink from her bottle of iced tea as he turned the heat up full blast. Michaelyn was making a final check of Julie's Toyota and getting ready to lock it up. He put the car in gear and rolled on past her until he was in front of the little mustang and stopped to wait for Michaelyn. Then rapidly, the night seemed to turn into day all around them.

The explosion was so loud Jacob felt pain in his ears. He tensed up, crushing the brake pedal, but the car jolted forward, skidding on the pavement. The fireball was so big behind them that it felt like sunburn on the back of his neck. Julie screamed, and her drink spilled out all over. Jacob looked back to see the Toyota sedan rotating in mid-air, completely engulfed in flames and finally hitting the ground on its roof. He stepped out into a cloud of oily smoke and shouted Michaelyn's name. Bits of the car were falling to earth as the fire roared so loud he could barely hear himself yelling. There was no sign of her. If she had been anywhere near the car, there was no way she could have survived.

Jacob shook, and his knees felt weak. What the hell happened? As the wind shifted, he watched a winding trail of vapor leading down to the truck lot below them. Someone had fired something at Julie's car. They were still in danger! His senses began to return to him as he heard the screams still coming from his car. He spun and dove back into the vehicle, fumbling to get it in gear and moving. There was foul smoke in the car. In shock, he had been breathing it in, and now a fit of coughing overcame him as he stared wide-eyed out the windshield and floored it. Jacob's Hyundai fishtailed past another small car, also moving fast toward the exit, and struck its fender. He hadn't seen it even though it was colored white. He heard something fall off the back of the car.

Looking to his left, he saw the familiar silhouette of the police-only Chevy. It wasn't moving. A muscle-bound man with a crew cut in a Carhart jacket was putting something in the trunk. Jacob drove on, careening to the onramp, jerking the wheel every few seconds as they hit small patches of ice, and he tried to correct.

He heard a crash behind them and looked back to see the assassin's vehicle had been struck broadside by the white car Jacob had just narrowly avoided. That would delay him, Jacob thought, but the police-only Chevy might be reinforced and still drivable. And whoever had been following them was very well equipped and manned. He had no doubt that they could hack into whatever GPS or anti-theft tracking system was installed in his rental car. They could still be in a lot of trouble. He made a mental note to learn more about such systems in the future if they survived all this. He skidded around a big rig that almost ran him down on its way out of the rest area, turned, and sped out onto I-90, the smoke from the Toyota still rising into the night sky behind him.

CHAPTER THIRTY-SIX

OPERATIONS CENTER

M3 cracked the door of M's office. A dim desk lamp glowed on one side of the room. On the other, the older man lay on a black leather couch with his back to the door. The office was large, about twice the size of M3's, and proportionate to M's rank as a department head. The décor, however, was completely different than the other executives' offices. Wood paneling lined the walls. His desk was expansive, made of thick, heavy mahogany. The floor was also wood, with several antique rugs, each marking a functional area. Along one wall, near the middle, was a fake fireplace with a wooden mantle and two wingback leather chairs. Opposite this area, were an analytic couch and a straight chair. At the far end was a large seating area, with two sofas and several chairs, all leather, flanked by a small kitchen area on one side and the door to a private bathroom on the other.

"Sir?" M3 shook M gently. His boss always wanted the straight truth right away, but M3 needed to make sure he was awake first. M turned and looked at M3, then sat up, rubbing his eyes. "Our man botched the termination. They're still on the move." M nodded. As M3 hurried away, M stared at the grandfather clock against the wall across from him. He could see it was sometime after midnight. His night assistant had entered the room and was walking toward him.

"A triple espresso, Wendy," he said to her as he slowly got to his feet and moved toward the bathroom. Wendy turned on some lights and went to the kitchen area to make M's coffee.

A few minutes later, M entered the Operations Center with his coffee, looking not so much rested and refreshed as maintained and preserved. No one else in the room had coffee or any food or drink whatsoever. Regulations strictly prohibited food and drinks in the Operations Center. Now, M3 was sitting in one of the big chairs on the back row, leaning forward, scanning the monitor wall and workstations in front of him. M joined him. "Sitrep," he said quietly to M3.

"All stations report. Let's update M. H?" M3 barked to the room.

"Our asset intercepted the system at a rest stop on I-90 near Fredonia, New York, where she was getting help from the target and a new unknown female. He attempted to destroy using an anti-tank weapon..."—M rolled his eyes and shook his head—"which destroyed the system's vehicle. However, the system was not confirmed terminated, and the target's vehicle was seen exiting the rest stop at high speed. Our asset was involved in a TA while trying to pursue. The targets escaped, and contact was broken." The H tech looked over at S.

"The system's vehicle was destroyed. The electronics stopped responding. There was another car, the photographer's replacement rental. He ditched his phone and even managed to disable the GPS on the vehicle. It had LoJack, but without involving law enforcement or military, it's impossible to locate without some excellent luck."

Next, it was the C tech's turn. "Calls made from the Fredonia stop around the time they were there include one to a Dr. Julius Green on Long Island." M3 was looking at M and noticed a hint of recognition.

"You know him?" queried M3.

"I've read him," said M. "He knows enough to help them. Christ, these guys are lucky."

A petite, pretty black woman from M department provided some background.

"Graduated summa cum laude, Johns Hopkins, 1976. Has written at least one article on the treatment of mind control victims and various other publications. Appears to have no specialty. Volunteers about a third of his time treating patients who can't afford therapy, many hours of VA service. Private practice in New York City since 1980." She had an inch-thick stack of printed material on the doctor and stood, waiting for any questions M or M3 might have.

"S is doing a satellite grid search for the car, but we won't have much to go on until daylight. By the time we've retask one of the synthetic aperture radar satellites, the sun will be up all over New York." M3 motioned toward the S workstation, around which hovered several techs. Some were working on laptops brought in and placed on top of the monitor enclosures of the permanent workstations. They were all paging through satellite photos, zooming in and out. "I?"

"Jacob posted an encrypted message to a blog. We're running it, but we're not going to find anything. We've been running that whole website all night. The messages are too short, they don't keep them up long, and they're using a non-standard key. It's not military. It could be anything, including something they wrote themselves." The I tech sat down and went back to watching his various consoles.

"We have Green's phone?" asked M.

"I'm on it," the C tech said, glancing back at M.

"Do we have anything else?" M sipped his espresso and motioned to the cute M tech for the Green documents.

"No. Other than the doctor, we don't know who they might call." M3 enviously looked at the cup of espresso in M's hand. Then he looked at the digital, multiple-time-zone clock at the top of the monitor wall. "H's asset is now on a forced vacation, just like our man in Toronto. He made too big of a splash at that rest area."

"Ya think?" M said sarcastically. M3 tried to hide a smile.

"I found the rental!" One of the S techs said. "It's at Snappy Car Rental, Chautauqua County-Dunkirk Airport."

"Double-check the airport for the target's rental car," said M3. "If it's not there, they probably didn't fly away." He got up and walked over to the S area.

M leaned back in his chair, trying to put himself in the minds of those he was hunting. He looked at the printout of an article called *Boot Camp Brainwashing: A Comparison of Military Training with Mind Control Programming*. The M tech was still standing next to him. "Do a full workup on our new female. Call her Target A.

And go back to what we have on the target, the photographer. Dig deeper. How does he know Green? Does he have any deprogramming skills, etc.," said M.

The girl nodded, walked back to her workstation, and picked up a phone, asking for the Hard Records Section. Cradling the receiver, she started typing at her workstation, then looked over at the S techs. "Can somebody get me a cap of the female's face from the rest stop?"

"Negative," responded the S tech sitting at his workstation. "Video was disabled – standard procedure prior to direct action by the H asset. I'll get someone to search traffic cam video compared with backtracked satellite video. The best bet will probably be Border Patrol."

"DMV on the car would be nice, too," said the M tech.

"We'll have it in about a minute."

CHAPTER THIRTY-SEVEN

BUFFALO

Josh looked around the room. Everyone was tired. He had rented a suite at the Hampton Inn. Julie got the bedroom to herself so she could rest as quietly as possible. His motley gang of video guerillas all flopped in couches, chairs, or on the floor. He had awakened Ty and Andreas after getting a call from an unknown number that turned out to be Jacob on a disposable phone. They had converged on this place in the middle of the night and collapsed for a few hours of restless darkness that could barely be called sleep. Ty had made coffee and started throwing questions at Josh as soon as Josh had gotten up, abandoning any hope of rest. Ty loved coffee. He thought that, surely, he would settle down soon.

"So, are we going to meet this Dr. Green?" asked Ty. "Have you ever met him?"

"He should be here by noon, I hope. No, Jacob knows him, but I don't think anyone else has ever seen him." Josh thought for a minute and sipped from a Hampton Inn coffee cup as he leaned against a wall in the tiny beige kitchen. He turned to Jacob, who was groping for a cup. "Do you think anyone followed you after you were attacked?"

"The guy who fired the missile,"—Jacob paused, a grim look overshadowing his countenance—"or whatever it was, was delayed, and I never saw him after we left the rest stop. But, you know, this is government or something big. With that kind of armament? At least three operatives, just counting the ones we know about. That CSIS agent was pretty cagey, too. I think she knew more than she let on. I wouldn't be sure which side she would be on, though. In any event, an organization like that is going to have serious resources. I think we have to assume they will be on top of us pretty soon."

"Absolutely," said Josh. "They don't know where we are. But they will eventually figure it out. I hope whoever came after Julie at that rest stop didn't know who you were. But if they know you, they'll eventually look for me. And if it's government, they'll have no trouble finding out I'm registered here as a guest."

"With that kind of weapon, that guy wanted to take out all three of us, which is why I'm pretty sure they don't know where we are now. If they did, they'd be coming after us, or at least Julie. It's a race now to see if they can take her out and us with her before we get her story to the public."

Josh could see the guilt and anguish Jacob was feeling. He gave his friend a look of sympathy and said, "We've never lost anyone like this."

"I just hope we get this film made," Jacob replied, "so her death will not have been in vain."

CHAPTER THIRTY-EIGHT

JULIUS

The practice of mind control is almost four thousand years old. In 1828, Jean-François Champollion and Ippolito Rosellini documented a scene from the tomb of Egyptian Pharaoh Seti I depicting, in one panel, a sorcerer or priest touching the head of a man. In subsequent panels, the sorcerer directs the man's movements from a distance. The original tomb painting dates from about 1279 BC.

In the twentieth century, between 1928 and 1977, miners discovered terra-cotta statues and objects near the modern Nigerian village of Nok. Based on the similarity of some of these artifacts to Egyptian gods and similar drawings in ancient Egyptian tombs and temples, archaeologists and sociologists connect this culture to the intermediate and late periods of ancient Egyptian cultural chronology. Some believe the two cultures communicated with one another.

Modern Vodun (known as *Voodoo* in the West) practitioners date the origins of their religion to Isis-worshipers. These former slaves, according to tradition, were known as *Yoruba* and worked constructing the pyramids before migrating south and merging with the Nok.

Voodoo spread to the West via the slave trade beginning around 1500 with its first appearance in Haiti. The practice of raising the dead, or making someone enter a death-like state, and controlling the corpse or body, is the earliest known form of mind control.

During the same period that the Yoruba labored in Egypt, practices of torture, intimidation, hypnotism, and the use of hallucinogenic drugs for the ritualized introduction of trauma to a victim were developed and documented in the *Book of the Dead*. The text was discovered in the Middle Ages and first published in modern form in 1805 by the staff of Napoleon's Egyptian expedition. This knowledge spread throughout the underground of European occult practitioners, who used it in their ritual abuse of humans alongside the practice of human sacrifice. The result of such practices was a kind of mental slavery.

When Hitler came to power in 1933, he immediately built the Dachau concentration camp, where hypnosis and pharmacology were studied as control mechanisms. Whether the Nazi military successfully used these techniques is unknown. However, American George Estabrooks claimed success in his mind control work with the U.S. military. His research at Colgate University resulted in the creation of hypnotically controlled agents for carrying classified messages to Japan and split personalities (known as *alters*) used to infiltrate Communist groups. This report appeared in an article in the April 1971 issue of Science Digest.

After World War II, some former Nazi scientists came to work for Soviet and US Intelligence agencies, continuing their mind-control technology development. A series of secret programs conducted by the National Security Council and the Central Intelligence Agency continued this work through the 1970s when the famous project MK-ULTRA was discontinued and most documentation destroyed. Many MK-ULTRA documents are now public, but little is known about one of its subprojects, MONARCH. This project was the one dealing directly with mind-control slavery. The details of this subproject remained classified.

Since the end of MK-ULTRA, no public information of any authority had come to light. Even the purpose and scope of MONARCH were still quite vague, and the only insights came from verbal accounts of former CIA employees, some of whom referred to the victims as computers programmed for specific tasks. Many speculating authors publish elaborate descriptions of systems and methods, claiming popular books, movies, and songs are used as triggering mechanisms for isolated alter-systems functioning as "sleepers" until called into nefarious action.

Such was the state of this field of study in 2011, as Dr. Julius Green piloted his 1980 BMW 325 up I-81 toward Syracuse. On the seat beside him was a file folder stuffed with documents, bound by a thick rubber band. He had brought his most recent programming and deprogramming research. Much of it was on his laptop in the trunk. However, as he drove through rush-hour traffic in a small town looking for gas and a restroom, the veteran psychiatrist didn't think he would have time to review this information, as the patient was waiting for him and in a delicate state. More significantly, she could be in physical danger as well.

After his last conversation with Michaelyn, Julius had said goodnight to his wife and driven to his Brentwood office. He was there for about an hour before receiving a call from Jacob's friend Josh asking if he could meet them upstate. He had been driving ever since.

Julius was a little concerned that what Jacob and his friends had done could be considered kidnapping and that even Julius might be an accessory. In his studies of brainwashing victims, he had encountered cult deprogrammers who had served hard time for this since they had taken adult cult members against their will, at least initially. Cult leaders had a vested interest in these prosecutions and had been successful in effectively stopping the practice of forced deprogramming since the 1980s, except for rescuing minors whose parents had consented to the rescue. He didn't think Jacob would take someone by force intentionally, and it was unclear who was after them. But Julius had long ago resigned himself to taking such risks. Doctors were highly intelligent, highly educated authority figures, and by necessity, risked accusations of abuse every time they entered a room alone with a patient. But to do any good, he had to take that risk every time.

CHAPTER THIRTY-NINE

NOTHIN'

The clock labeled New York said 12:01 in red digits. It was one of twelve time displays all mounted together horizontally on the Operations Center's front wall, each representing a different time zone. M3 sat alone in one of the oversized chairs on the elevated platform at the back of the room. He stared at the clock. His tie was tight around his neck. His shirt still looked perfectly pressed. But his face displayed a look of determined frustration.

He looked around the room. The lighting was always subdued to make the monitors and display screens easier to see. Some of the computer workstations were locked with an NSA screensaver. The giant projection monitors at the front of the room were divided into multiple displays that could be changed and moved around. There was a small square in the upper left with a news channel playing, muted. Another showed The Weather Channel. To the right was a large square that showed a dark map focused on the Northeastern US. A blinking red dot showed the last location of Julie Foley and Jacob.

As M3 stared at the dot, it seemed to grow and blink faster. He pictured a face on the dot laughing at him. His frustration only drove him to a more intense focus on the task at hand. Perhaps he needed to take an additional risk. He stood and walked over to the M station. He picked up the phone there and pressed a speed-dial button. The red dot from the jumbo screen seemed to irritate him like the burning sun irradiating sensitive skin.

"Who's in the room right now?" he inquired. "Okay, you meet me in my office now."

M3 arrived at his office door at the same time as M31, a slim, thirty-ish woman with a scrubbed look, her hair up, wearing a white shirt and black skirt and carrying a note pad and a thick file folder. He held the office door for her as they walked in and sat. "Have we missed anything? Have we looked at every minute detail of the records on this system? 'Cause right now, we got nothin'."

M31 was the senior technician on duty. Ostensibly, she was responsible for ongoing systems development, but as the top tech, she would also be keeping tabs on the department's key activities through the weekend shift. M3 expected that she had reviewed everything the records library had on Julie, spoken with the library techs, and compiled the latest communications and reports. She also had received training on the various possible scenarios based on likely moves any system might make if something went wrong. Eventually, something always went wrong. Sometimes it was something inconsequential. This was not one of those times.

"She's left her range," said M31. "The behavior is unexpected, mainly because she's under the influence of people we barely know."

"Is it the backstop?" he asked. "Did we miss something there?"

"I think the backstop is pretty solid," said M31 confidently, glancing at a page deep in the pages of the file folder. "She was young enough, still in adolescent prefrontal cortical development. CT scans showed 75% of adult density. The story appears to be complete, but I'm not an expert on backstop narratives. Still, we had to take a girl out of Arkansas and put her in Canada somehow. Might have been a challenge."

"So, tell me something new." M3 sometimes called in a subordinate merely to vent his frustration, as much as he tried to hide the fact.

But in his mind, it was an attempt at something constructive. He knew that two heads were better than one. It's the only reason people still came to buildings to work together. Non-verbal communication was just as important as all the data moving through cables and airwaves put together. Two people in a room together. A sum that was greater than its parts. That's what M3 thought as his colleague's words bounced off his backhanding brain.

"Jacob isn't one of our systems. And even H and I departments have only light info on the guy." She opened her folder and pulled out a summary printout with a couple of pages stapled to it. "A resume. A bunch of YouTube videos produced in between larger projects. We've been watching all of those, but they're looking out, not looking in. Politicians, bankers, masons. Not people he associates with. He never films himself. He's been on some radio and TV but mostly leaves that to others." M31 looked away and closed the file folder.

M3 quickly looked up from the papers and held his hand up as if to stop her. "What others?"

"Josh Aidan," she said as if M3 should already know.

"Rings a bell. So?"

"Small-time producer or something," M31 continued. "Made a splash with one of those

9/11 conspiracy viral videos." She still looked bored and sounded dismissive. Everything she was telling her boss had been kicked around multiple times while he was in the Operations Center with M.

"Check it out," M3 ordered, nodding, pointing, acting as if he had discovered something important.

"Really? That was years ago."

"Yes. Now. Find out where he is, get a man on him. Get his credit cards, phones, car, everything. We have assets sitting around, waiting for Jacob or Julie to pop up. They can track this guy for a while." M31 stood up. "One more thing. Do you have a contact at the Bureau?"

The corners of M31's mouth turned up in a look of self-disappointment. In any large organization, there were official channels of communication with the outside world. These channels were for the benefit of the organization, not those outside of it. This was true of corporations and their small shareholders, businesses and their customers, certainly, government agencies and citizens they served, but most especially, intelligence agencies. If you didn't have a personally developed contact, you didn't have anything. M31 had been around long enough to know this, but being a more bookish and analytical person, M3 wasn't sure she had been able to develop many contacts of value in other agencies.

"Just someone in IT," she said.

"Time to parlay that into something of value. Get what you can on our Mr. Aidan." She got up and hurried out of the room. "I'll send the alert out to man the OC. I want you and your librarian in there," he called out. M31 nodded as she jogged down the hallway.

1:05 PM. Operations Center. It was standing room only. Some techs stood in front of the consoles working on laptops. The air was filled with stressed murmurs and whispers as each team worked to put together the information available on Josh. M3 paced at one side of the room, rolling up his sleeves. The number of bodies in the room had raised its temperature by five degrees. He watched everything. He listened to the chatter. He knew they would all continue working until he asked a question or until someone located Josh.

Everyone acted excited to be in the OC, but no one really wanted it. It was much more comfortable to be sitting in a cubicle quietly doing work, listening to music, drinking a soda, and most importantly, enjoying an illusion of privacy. At the rare times when no manager was present, there was still the wall of windows at the back of the room. The windows could be darkened for security but were often kept clear on the weekends. And there was video and audio that managers could remotely view. Some called this room "the fishbowl."

M3 walked over to the S station. The young tech looked up and said, "He hasn't been seen around his apartment in the last twenty-four hours." M3 nodded, showing no approval or encouragement. Across the room, M31 eyed him warily, standing behind the M station.

"Are you sure that's his apartment?" M3 asked, just loud enough for the whole room to hear him. He stared at the live satellite picture of a high-rise apartment building.

"It's one possible address," M31 answered. "He has a driver's license, but no vehicles are registered in his name or his company's name."

M3 smiled at her with approval as she walked toward him. "Good work. What else did you get from the FBI?" He scanned a printed summary as the I tech raised his hand.

"Uh, Sir? He used a credit card last night."

CHAPTER FORTY

THREE SIMPLE KNOCKS

" There's not full coverage," said Thompson. He was sitting back on the couch, eyes fixed on the screen of Jacob's laptop. "We just have to go from gate to gate." Jacob was scanning through video files of Logan Airport security video. Thompson's contact had been highly cooperative, taking him to a storage area where he found all of the security video from September 11, 2001. Not wanting to take a lot of his contact's time, Thompson had borrowed all of the tapes from that day, vowing to return them as soon as possible. Josh contacted a Boston firm that specialized in digitizing all kinds of data, especially video. The team spent that night prioritizing the tapes for digitizing, starting with gate B32 and the gates near it. B32 was the gate from which American Airlines flight 11 had departed.

When the manager of the digitizing firm arrived the next morning, Thompson had greeted him warmly with a cup of coffee and a carload of VHS tapes. The manager had agreed to return with the batch marked "Priority" as soon as they were completed and follow up with the others later. He also promised to have someone work on them until all of the tapes were converted, continuing after closing if necessary. The first batch had been delivered, and Thompson and Jacob were now sifting through them.

Jacob, the consummate professional, was viewing the video with Thompson, but he was also organizing and editing at the same time, saving clips that showed promise, so, at the end of the first viewing, he would have something rough to work with, though it would likely change significantly as they learned more.

Despite all the precautions and codes that had become a part of life for Josh and his crew, Dr. Julius Green's arrival was announced only by three simple knocks at the door of the hotel room where most of them had been encamped for the previous ten hours. He was let in by Ty, who introduced himself and the others who had come to life around the room, now filled with light from the two large windows facing the eastern side of the Hampton Inn. Josh broke the news to him of the rest stop attack and

Michaelyn's death. All were silent for a moment, and Dr. Green showed signs of nervousness. Like the others, he was coming to grips with the magnitude of the forces against them.

"Well, how is our girl?" the doctor asked, looking around the room for a female.

Josh motioned toward the bedroom door. "She had a very stressful night, as you know, but slept when she got here. She's up now, though. You can see her whenever you are ready." Julius looked at the small desk near the kitchen area.

"Jacob and I have been checking on her," Josh offered. "She's watching TV. She hasn't spoken much, but I think she's going to be curious soon about what happens next."

Josh felt a mood of concern for Julie in the room. Though they all had good intentions, Julie was vulnerable. If their situation were not so desperate, it would not be right to keep her there.

"I hope you can help her," he said.

"That mostly depends on Julie now. She is probably just leaning on you now." Seeing no one at the desk, he motioned toward it and looked at Josh, who gestured approvingly. Julius carefully set down his folder on the desk and put his laptop on the floor. "I would like a little time to organize," he said, sitting down.

Ty walked in the door to the suite with a couple of bags of groceries and some newspapers. "Lunchtime! Who's hungry?" he asked, removing his sunglasses and setting the room's keycard on the kitchen counter.

Julius raised a finger and said, "Cup of coffee, please," not looking up from his work.

"Coming up!" said Ty, dumping some old coffee out of a pot and washing it out.

Dressed in a pair of jeans, a black t-shirt with a white line drawing on the front, and socks with no shoes, Julie sat in a chair with her feet on the bed. She was lucid, with a bored look on her face. Her hair was pulled back in a ponytail, and she held the TV remote. Josh poked his head into the room after knocking softly. "Julius is here. Everyone is having lunch. Are you hungry?" He opened the door a little and stepped into the doorway, leaning against its frame.

Julie looked downward, considering the question. Then she looked up, confident of her decision. "Yes." She started to get up.

"I can bring you something if you like," said Josh. Julie had not left the bedroom since she arrived. It would be a big step for her and everyone else.

"No," Julie said with determination. "I need to get out of this room and see what's going on."

As she walked through the door where Josh had just been standing, Julie looked around. All eyes turned to her as silence fell. Julius looked up from his desk with a look of surprise. Thompson and Jacob looked around, and Jacob started to smile. Julie's face betrayed not so much discomfort as dismay at the weirdness of it. She thought, "What are they all looking at?" but said nothing.

Ty was the first one to break the ice. "Good afternoon, ma'am! I have a table reserved for you in the kitchen if you'll walk this way." He set a steaming cup of coffee on the desk near Julius's hand and dropped a couple of creamer cups near it. Julius displayed a growing, pleased smile. Julie smiled a little and took Ty's hand as he led her to the serving counter. "More of a barstool," Ty continued, "but it's the best we have, really. Can I get you something to drink?"

As Ty whipped up some frozen pizza and Julie drank a Coke, the room went back to normal for a while. Julius approached Julie and introduced himself. "Are you the guy that's going to fix me?"

Julius drained his coffee cup as he got comfortable on the stool next to Julie and said: "I hope that I can help you make sense of what you're feeling." The job of the therapist involved speaking little and listening much.

As Ty served his first lunch customer a slice of pepperoni pizza, Julius pointed at her food and then at himself. "Comin' right up!" Ty said. He was relishing his role as a short-order cook.

Julius turned to Julie, "We both need a little nourishment before we get into the details."

Julie nodded. "I can't believe how hungry I was!"

Josh set down two cups of coffee on the table near where Julie and Julius sat in the bedroom. They were facing each other, sitting almost knee-to-knee. Julie's eyes were focused on the doctor's face as he spoke clearly and correctly to her. Josh wondered what it was all about as he pulled the bedroom door shut.

A cell phone rang somewhere on the other side of the living area. "Yeah," Thompson answered. He looked at Jacob, still working on the laptop, then turned to Josh. "They have the rest of the video done. Should I go grab it?"

Josh was standing by the entryway, holding a can of Coke. He looked at his cell phone. "It's Saturday. Is Pete available?"

"Not as far as his wife is concerned," Thompson laughed.

"Try him," said Josh. He looked at Jacob, thinking of Michaelyn's husband and Jacob's friend Steve. Under normal conditions, Josh would have asked Steve to help. He couldn't imagine what Steve was feeling after the sudden death of his wife.

Josh began pacing, thinking. The crew was in good spirits. Julius was working. It was now a race for time. How fast would Julie be ready to go on camera? How long would they be safe here?

CHAPTER FORTY-ONE

HER TROUBLED MIND

"I think we need to pull back the curtains and get full sunlight," Jacob said, looking up from the LCD screen of his camera, now on a tripod facing one end of the small living area of the hotel room.

"Okay, but it's gonna glare up," Ty responded.

"You're right. I don't think it will be too much, though, if we put Julie in the soft chair toward the corner. That way, the sunlight is indirect." Ty and Jacob began moving around furniture to get things just right.

Outside, Julie was taking a walk around the hotel, accompanied by Josh. She had wanted to get some fresh air. Even though the temperature was in the forties, it was a welcome change from the stale humidity of the cramped hotel room. The sun was shining now, and the building broke the wind coming off Lake Erie down to a gentle draft. Josh was there for Julie's protection and peace of mind. And Josh needed to prepare Julie for the difficult task ahead of her. The pressure of a video interview was draining, even for a well-rested person in normal circumstances. For Julie, it would be that much more of a challenge.

"I know you are still raw from the discoveries you've been making with Julius," Josh said, pulling his ungloved hands out of his pockets briefly to talk with his hands. But the frigid air had him quickly shoving them back in his jacket pockets for warmth. Julie nodded. "And you probably want to just go back to your family and just *be* for a while."

"But I can't, right?" Josh stared ahead as he listened. In a way, Julie knew more about what was going on than anyone. Somewhere in her troubled mind was the story, answers to questions Josh wanted to explain and show to the world. But she needed help to get those answers out.

Josh nodded and continued. "I know you have been through an ordeal, and you need more than just a couple of hours with Julius to get through it." Josh lightly touched her shoulder, and she didn't recoil. But he still had no gloves and quickly returned his hand to his jacket. "We want you to get that help and to have that time. My concern is that if we don't get as much of the story as we can recorded now, something might happen that would keep us from ever getting it. And that's important…"—Josh had his hands out now, damn the cold—"because the people chasing us most certainly won't do anything to you once the world knows what happened."

"And we can't call the police."

"No," said Josh, "We can't. Not right now. They mean well, but if we go in, whoever is chasing us—my guess is somebody from the intelligence structure—will know exactly where to find us, and the police won't know any better than to escort them right to us. No, we need people to look at the whole story, see the pictures, and believe you are who you say you are."

"I had fingerprints taken once," Julie said. She was now entirely on board, helping as much as possible.

"You rob a bank or something?" Josh laughed, and even Julie smiled.

"No," Julie answered, smiling. "Just worked at a daycare center when I was a teenager." They joked about this as they headed for the door and the warmth inside the Hampton Inn.

Inside, Jacob, who now seemed happy with the setup, put on a small headset attached to a radio on his belt. Meanwhile, Andreas had arrived and was speaking to Julius.

"I know you have an obligation of confidentiality with her," Andreas said, "but she is willing to be open. Why can't you just give me your notes?"

"Well, I can't tell you everything we talked about," said Julius, "but most of it wouldn't interest you anyway. My job is to help Julie understand who she is and who she was. Your job is to find out what happened. Those are questions you'll have to ask her anyway. What I can tell you is that she doesn't know the whole story, and there are still gaps in her memory about her part in it."

"We'll do the best we can," said Andreas, nodding. "You're going to be around?"

"Certainly, I need to be here for Julie in case she needs me." Andreas seemed satisfied with that and went to speak with Julie, who had just returned from her brief walk outside with Josh.

"Okay, we're ready," said Jacob. He gently guided Julie to her seat in the corner. Andreas was seated across from her on the couch, which had been dragged into the middle of the room and turned to face the corner.

NSA Operations Center. "None of the agents have responded," said the C tech. "We've been having problems with the biometric authentication system, so that may be what is slowing them down."

"Then send a message in the clear, damn it! I want bodies all over that hotel," M3 was a wreck. He had been babysitting this operation all week. He usually kept to his weekend shift, but this was the most significant case he had ever seen.

An H tech stood up to face M3. "If you want that kind of response, we need to get the FBI involved. We only have two or three agents, and a couple of them are hours away by car."

A grave look came over M3's face. "That would be like going public."

"Any convergence of a bunch of agents on a hotel is going to take this public. And there is an FBI field office right in Buffalo with over 100 agents."

"Do it. I'll call the big boss." M3 picked up the secure phone in the back of the Operations Center. He would call M. Then he would call the Deputy Director for Operations. Neither of them would be happy. But they needed to be prepared for the potential media storm that would follow.

The indications were straightforward: As long as Josh Aiden didn't get to the press, they could make up any story they wanted. If he did make his own splash, they would need to discredit him. Only one thing was absolutely certain. Julie Foley had to be eliminated. She wasn't supposed to exist, and as far as anyone outside the NSA knew, she didn't exist and never would again. She could never be allowed to appear in public to corroborate the story Aiden was trying to tell.

CHAPTER FORTY-TWO

JULIE'S STORY

"There was a man." Julie was almost lost in her thoughts, trying to recollect the past. It was a past that didn't want to be recalled, that hid in the nooks and crannies of her brain, behind symbols she did not understand. Julius had helped her disregard some of those symbols as irrelevant to reveal the actual events recorded in her mind. But it wasn't easy. "I know there was one man that I spent an extraordinary amount of time with."

"Let's return to the beginning," Andreas said, steering the interview back to its true path. "You said that everyone was taken off the airplane and taken to a large room."

"It was a converted hangar," Julie recalled, nodding. "I could tell because, on one wall, there were seams where the main doors had been."

Years of airport experience came to bear as she dredged up details of the incident. "I was based out of Dallas. I wasn't familiar with the airport."

September 12, 2001. 1 a.m. The aircraft's cabin was dark, except for a red glow coming from the front, the flight attendants' area behind the curtain. Derrick stood in the galley, pouring water into cups on a cart. He wore white pants and a white smock, like a nurse or a lab tech. Into each cup, he also poured something from a small plastic cup that looked like the kind that comes with bottles of cough syrup. He looked up as the lights came on. "Good morning," a friendly female voice said over the PA system. "We will be arriving at our destination soon." Derrick wondered if she had been trained in how to lie in such an unthreatening way. The plane had taken off from Cleveland just twenty minutes earlier. The passengers were exhausted from being isolated all day and all night. The point was to wake them up, so he could drug them, ensuring that they wouldn't talk amongst themselves until they could be programmed. He turned his cart down the aisle and began distributing the water, making a note of those who refused or wanted coffee or something else.

Julie sat in the front row of first-class, across from the two pilots of the original flight out of Boston. She woke up, still tired and now thirsty. She drank the cup of water offered to her. Then, darkness.

Julie awoke to a gentle nudge from Derrick. "Come this way, please." As she followed him toward the main hatch, she wondered what Derrick was. She had never seen a flight attendant dressed that way. And he was wearing work boots. Derrick stepped aside and motioned for her to step out onto a movable staircase. The airliner stood inside a dimly lit, closed hangar. The only open door was a garage door in the wall to her right, in front of the airplane. At the bottom of the staircase, a limousine was parked with its rear passenger door open. A man in a suit with a driver's cap looked up toward her as if waiting for her. "Where are we going?" she asked him.

"This is just for your security, ma'am." Julie looked past the driver's ear to the walk-in door on the wall behind the aircraft. A man dressed in black military fatigues was standing there with his arms crossed.

"Where are we?" she asked the driver as she stepped into the vehicle.

"Ask the man inside," he replied.

The door slammed shut, and she caught a glimpse of a man in the darkness sitting across from her. Then it was gone.

Julie shuddered and stopped speaking suddenly. "What's wrong? Are you okay?" asked Andreas.

"No, I guess I'm fine. I just don't remember anything else about that car ride." But she was visibly upset, folding her arms tightly and tucking her chin into her chest. "Can I have a glass of water, please?" Ty shot off to the kitchen while Jacob continued to watch the LCD screen on his camera. In the bedroom next door, Josh sat at the desk, which they had pulled in from the other room. On it was Jacob's laptop, streaming video of the interview wirelessly from the camera.

"What was *that*?" Josh asked Julius, who was sitting next to him.

"I said there would be gaps," Julius replied. "Some of them may be placeholders for traumatic events."

"Such as?"

"If she was brainwashed," Julius said, with a hint of skepticism, "the initiation ritual would most likely involve sexual trauma."

"You mean she was raped?" Josh looked at the screen as Julie was standing up, stretching, and drinking her water.

"Or seduced, or exposed to something sexual or otherwise shocking that caused her trauma." Julius leaned back and pointed his finger for emphasis. "The reason it would be sexual is that in our culture, at least, it evokes the emotion of shame, which enforces secrecy. And secrecy is the key to mind control. Secrecy from the victim's self, and secrecy from anyone who could help her."

Josh shook his head, eyes fixed on the monitor. "Sick bastards."

Julius nodded. "Indeed."

"Do you remember anything after that?" Andreas asked Julie.

"Just vague images of a warehouse full of animal cages, like a zoo or something."

"Is that where you got out of the car?"

"No," Julie replied. "It was a large, square house with lots of windows and several floors and a circular drive in front. There was nothing around it for miles. But that's just another image. I don't remember any people or doing anything, just seeing the house."

Andreas shifted his focus. "You lived in Toronto for a while, right?"

"That's where this all started, yeah. So, I must have been there for ten years." Julie acknowledged the missing sections in her memory but seemed annoyed because of them.

"What is your first memory of being there?"

"Well, I just remember being in my apartment one day. I got out of bed on a Saturday morning and immediately went to my computer." She shook her head again as her story unfolded. She had said these things were coming back to her, things she had forgotten for years. She remembered things about herself that she had failed to notice as they happened. "I never really cared that much about computers. That seems strange now. But that was a pretty normal occurrence, even on weekends."

"What about the next Monday morning? Did you go to work at Emerald Financial?"

"Yes. I don't remember working anywhere else in Toronto."

"Your resume says you are a Certified Investment Advisor. Do you remember ever training for that?" Andreas now had papers spread out to his left and right on the couch. He held the resume in his hand.

"No," said Julie. "I just was one. Not only did I know what I needed to know, but I was interested in finance and enjoyed the job. I had never had an interest in that before."

"Did you ever encounter someone strange in your life, that didn't seem to belong, or that had any kind of unexplained familiarity?" Andreas seemed desperate for anything at this point.

Julie paused in thought for a few seconds. "Someone strange. You mean *other* than Jacob?" They both laughed.

"Yes, other than him."

"No one approached me directly," she replied, "but once my boss told me someone had called asking for me. Maybe just checking to see if I was there. I don't know. I never heard anything more about him, but I do remember the name. Gerhardt. Not a very common name in Toronto. But who knows if it was his real name. He asked for me specifically, though. Then he hung up before the receptionist could transfer the call."

"Go on in," said the receptionist, with a knowing look. The man she spoke to was middle-aged and wore glasses. He looked like a college professor and carried a briefcase. He gave the receptionist a look of reproach, then walked past the Emerald Financial logo emblazoned on the wall behind her, a short distance down a hallway. He seemed to know exactly where he was going as if he did it regularly. Opening the door, he entered, looking Julie right in the eyes. She did not recognize him, although she had seen him many times before.

The room was windowless, with abstract art on neutral-colored walls. The table was large enough to seat eight to ten people, but there were only two chairs: the one Julie sat in and the empty one across the table from it. The man took the empty chair and immediately began to work. "Grace tackle," said the man. Suddenly Julie acted as if she knew him and was no longer suspicious. "I am Gerhardt. We have a bit of work to do today, Julie."

After Gerhardt left, Julie never remembered he had been there.

"When was this call by Gerhardt?" asked Andreas.

"Early," Julie told him, "probably about 2003. Just after Christmas."

"Let's go back to 9/11," said Andreas. "When did you find out what had happened and what they said about your flight in the media?"

"I didn't really know any of that until much later. I was already in Toronto, and it was a TV special, I think an anniversary or something. The war in Iraq was already going on. I remember that."

"You talked briefly about the man who gave you instructions in Boston. Did he tell you anything about the attacks?" Asking the same questions in different ways was a tried and true research technique. First, you ask, then you ask again. After a time, you ask again. Andreas knew that sometimes several interviews with the same person asking for basically the same information would yield a variety of answers and more truth. The mind works through connections.

Julie took a deep breath and let it out. Andreas knew she was trying very hard. But it was a tiring exercise. It would be better if they didn't have to do this interview in one day. The sun warmed the room and glowed on her arm and the side of her face. Trying to relax, she closed her eyes.

"He told me that there had been a terrorist attack and that the FAA had grounded all flights," Julie said. "He said that we would all be put on a military flight and taken to safety because there might be other attacks on the East Coast. But he said it was important not to call anyone on the phone or communicate in any way."

"Did he say why you couldn't call your family?" Andreas asked.

"He said the government was scrambling to find out how this attack happened and that domestic espionage was suspected. He made me believe that spies were everywhere, and I could trust no one. Now it's embarrassing that I believed him. But at the time, his explanations made perfect sense."

"Do you have any idea how they knew enough to take you off the flight and why no other flights had been unloaded?"

"Well," said Julie, "I got the impression that as enormous a task as it would be, everyone would go through the same thing I was going through. Looking back, it is unbelievable, but the situation that whole day was unbelievable. In that context, I think I would have believed almost anything. I had no reason to believe I was being lied to."

"Julie, it seems you were alone or with one official for a long time. Did you see or talk to anyone else that was on the flight?"

"Yes, in the beginning." Andreas knew this process was difficult for Julie, but it was working. But where would all this lead?

CHAPTER FORTY-THREE

FBI

" don't know what you guys are up to. And I don't like not knowing." Bill Forman, the Special Agent In Charge of the Buffalo Field Office of the FBI, was no idiot. How many times had the various government and military agencies gotten in trouble domestically and had the FBI take all the heat, do the cleanup, and take the blame? He was not going to be the scapegoat this time. If he sent his people in to apprehend someone holed up in a hotel in broad daylight, he wanted to know who and why. And, he wanted to be absolutely certain it wasn't going to blow back on him.

M3 sounded urgent, but Forman could tell he wasn't telling the whole story. "It's tantamount to a foreign incursion, Bill. These guys have classified information about ongoing operations, and they are about to go public."

"What information?" Bill was also sensitive to something going awry in his backyard *without* his involvement.

"Classified information." M3 was not going for it.

"Look, if it's an invasion, call the National Guard," Forman said. "I can transfer you to the 153rd Troop Brigade. Just keep me in the loop." One way or another, Bill would get some idea of what was going on, find out how desperate the NSA was, and why.

M3 paused.

"Okay," he said. "We screwed up. We should have involved you guys earlier."

"No shit." Bill smiled in victory.

"We had a foreign asset that went off the reservation—a Canadian. I just want you to hold them until one of our agents can get there and take custody. Don't interrogate them. We'll take care of all that."

Downstairs at the FBI's Buffalo Field Office, Liam leaned on the front desk while the guard called the SAIC's office. He looked around, wondering how he ever got in this position. One day he was getting handcuffed for stealing credit card numbers on the Internet. The next day he was working for the U.S. government, with a paycheck and everything. He wasn't sure if he was the fool or if they were. He supposed it was just a relationship of mutual benefit, sealed by mutual secrecy.

"Okay, your escort will be here shortly. You can wait in one of those chairs." The guard smiled and hung up the phone. Liam nodded thanks, shouldered his backpack, and turned toward the chairs. But he never got there. An agent was already walking quickly out of the elevator toward him.

"Fisk," A man said, walking up to Liam.

"Liam." Liam shook hands with Fisk, who was wearing a white shirt, black tie, and an armored vest. He turned toward the guard.

"I need a level three badge for him," Fisk said to the guard. Then, turning to Liam, "I'll be staying with you the whole way." He took a visitor badge on a lanyard and gave it to Liam, who put it on over his head as they started walking toward the other side of the building from the elevator from which Fisk had emerged.

"I'm taking you to the Special Agent in Charge. We're already prepping for the raid. I assume you have some information for us?" Liam smirked. All detectives and investigators are trained to get as much information as possible in any way possible. It wasn't Fisk's job to know, but he would ask anyway. He was a cop. It was just in his nature.

"Yeah, I'll give a briefing to whoever needs it once we get with the SAIC." Liam was just a contract agent. He really shouldn't have been there. But then, it could be said that no one associated with the NSA should have been. Their charter was for foreign surveillance. He had photos of Julie, Josh, Jacob, Michaelyn (from a border surveillance camera), and Julius. The NSA didn't know about Andreas or Ty. He would give them the photos to copy for all the agents and tell them they were all foreign spies or collaborators.

What a story, Liam thought. Those NSA guys could sell Bibles in Hell if they wanted to. The subjects were to be apprehended and detained but not questioned. Liam would be their shepherd until they could be transported by the NSA for further interrogation, after which, supposedly, they would be deported or brought to trial, depending on their status. In reality, Liam knew that neither of these would ever be allowed to happen. His employer was extremely risk-averse when it came to information. Information was controlled. People with knowledge were either blackmailed, like Liam, or imprisoned, if useful, or killed. Then there was Julie Foley. Liam wasn't sure what category she fit in, but he did not envy her. She did not have a bright future, whatever they decided to do with her.

Forty minutes later, Liam was in the back of an FBI sedan with Bill Forman in the front passenger seat. Fisk was driving like a madman, chirping tires at every turn, punching it through every traffic light.

CHAPTER FORTY-FOUR

INTERRUPTED

September 11, 2001. 8:30 a.m. A perky, young Julie Foley smiled big at the few passengers that walked on. Some of them, she knew by name from seeing them every week. Flight 11 was an institution, a regular trans-continental flight for many years. Passengers would arrive in Los Angeles with a full workday ahead of them due to the time difference. But it was often no more than half-full, which made it a popular run with flight attendants. Greeting the commuters with a smile, Julie jabbed her elbow into the ribs of Terry, the co-pilot, who was getting a little too close behind her. He did little things like this all the time, thinking it was a joke, but the young lady from Arkansas never welcomed his physical advances. She never reported it, but she wasn't afraid to fight back.

"Bravo 32, Central." A voice crackled over several handheld radios carried by baggage carriers.

"Bravo 32, go ahead." The check-in clerk answered the call at the other end of the jetway.

"I need you to complete check-in, then send all passengers and crew with Officer Lindstrom."

"All passengers are checked in," said the clerk, obviously annoyed that the last thirty minutes of work would be wasted. "Why? What's going on?"

"All I know is what I told you. Bernie's on the way. He should be there. He knows where to take 'em. Out."

Julie looked at her crew leader, who shook her head. This was a new one. If it was a security or maintenance problem that required deboarding, they usually just waited in the terminal for the issue to be resolved or moved to a different gate. But it didn't matter. Airport security was part of the job, so they all grabbed their luggage and started down the jetway.

"You can leave your luggage, folks," said Bernie Lindstrom, walking up toward them, just far enough into the passageway to give them the word. "I was told to ask you to please leave everything on the plane." He turned and walked back. Julie and the others did as they were told.

"Pieces of luggage and clothing were found in the wreckage at Ground Zero," Andreas informed Julie, "but no identifiable human remains of the passengers and crew."

"Thank God," said Julie.

"Julie, I know this is difficult," Andreas began, giving her time to brace for another deep probe. "Think back to when you awoke on the airplane, and they took you out into that dark hangar." Andreas paused again, taking it easy and slow. "You said that you had a flash of recollection, an image of a man. Try to recall this image. His face, everything you can remember from that image." Julie was starting to shut down again but fought it, gripping the square arms of her chair. "Have you ever seen that man anywhere else?"

In her mind, an image of a dark door appeared. Julie was afraid of what was behind it. The door wasn't locked. But she wished it was. She heard screams from behind it. The screams were her own. And she heard the voice of a man. Suddenly she put her head down in her hands and started to sob. Jacob took off his headset and ran around the camera and the couch, kneeling in front of her.

"We're done," he said. "Let's get out of here."

"No." Julie held up her hand and slowly raised her head, wiping tears from her cheeks. Ty handed her a Kleenex. "No, let's keep going," she said. Jacob looked doubtful but quickly rose and returned to his station behind the camera, hitting the button to start recording a new 5-minute clip. "He was the man I spent most of my time with."

"Go on," Andreas carefully urged her.

"I don't know. I have to fight my memory because it's confused with someone else. I know it's the same man, but the picture in my mind says it is someone else. His face, but not his body." Julie sniffed and blew her nose.

"Can you describe him? How old was he?"

In the next room, Josh and Julius sat with eyes locked on the laptop screen. Josh looked at Julius and smiled. He was pleased and amazed. He didn't think they would be getting this kind of information so soon.

Julie leaned back in the chair, squeezing the used Kleenex in her hand. "He was in his fifties, heavyset. He had a full head of hair, brown and only slightly greying. He wore glasses and usually a three-piece suit."

"Did you see him in the place that you said looked like a 'zoo'?" Andreas pushed.

Julie closed her eyes, placed her hands on either side of her head, and shook it from side to side. It was a painful memory.

"I saw him there every day," she said. "He spent time at every cage almost every day."

"What kind of animals were there?"

"The cages didn't contain animals."

CHAPTER FORTY-FIVE

TEN TWENTY-SIX

J osh stood up to stretch his legs. They were still recording in the next room, sending video to the laptop, storing it in a series of files on an external hard drive. The drive light blinked rapidly as the data ran across these connections to the spinning disk inside. He walked to the window as Julius gazed intently at the monitor and picked up Josh's headset to listen closer. At the window, Josh's eyes grew wide, and he froze in fear at what he saw in the parking lot.

"Get out of here, Julius. Go home." Josh was picking up the headset to speak to Jacob. "Jake, go to thirty-second clips. We're cutting it close." He turned back to Julius, who was still sitting at the desk, a look of alarmed ignorance on his face. "Go!" Josh shouted, pulling Julius out of his chair by the arm. "Now! They're coming!"

Julius obeyed this time. He grabbed his coat and briefcase and walked for the door.

"We're at the back," Forman barked into a radio. "Take a station at the front. Have Burkhardt set up a perimeter at the property line. Check traffic out against the photos, and let no traffic in." Forman's assistant acknowledged his orders. Forman was standing by the open door to his sedan. He buttoned his FBI windbreaker against the wind in the afternoon sun. Liam exited the back seat and stood up behind him. He also wore an FBI windbreaker and baseball cap, borrowed for the occasion. His instructions had included a warning that the subjects could have weapons and were unpredictable and could be dangerous. Forman hoped that would not make his people have itchy trigger fingers.

Julius heard tires screeching as he started his car. A stream of black sedans and SUVs were entering the parking lot in front of the hotel, where he had parked when he arrived a few hours earlier. Julius never thought to park somewhere else. He didn't think anyone would be looking for him.

He still was not sure anyone was looking for him, specifically, so he decided to chance driving out. But by the time he got to the parking lot exit, a man was stationed there with a radio. The man motioned for Julius to stop as he held the radio to his ear. Julius lowered the driver's side window of his car.

"Let 'em in, but not out? Got it." The man was dressed in the FBI uniform: black suit pants, white shirt, black tie. He wore body armor with a windbreaker over it and a black FBI baseball cap. He was turning to Julius when something else crackled over the radio. "This is Burkhardt. Say again?"

The order came back clear enough for Julius to hear it. "Check ... against ... the ... photos."

"Copy," he said into the radio. And then to Julius, "I'm sorry, sir. Just one moment." The agent reached into his jacket and brought out an envelope from which he withdrew a stapled package of photocopy sheets. Julius tensed as he waited. Then he saw photos of Julie and Michaelyn as the agent flipped them over. He stopped at one of the pictures, then looked at Julius more seriously. "Sir, please turn off the engine." Julius complied.

"This is Burkhardt. Ten Twenty-Six at the front parking lot entrance, over." Julius heard more voices on the radio as the agent opened his door. "Step out of the vehicle, please, sir."

"I parked at the coffee shop across Delaware," said Ty. "I think that's the best chance we have."

"Then give Jake your keys," said Josh. "They're going to be coming in real soon, but we may have some time. They should know we won't be armed, but they still have to be a little cautious anyway."

Jacob was looking out the window of the living area. "Definitely feds. No uniforms, no rollers. Should we call the police?"

"Hell, yes," said Josh. "Call nine-one-one, but first, let me get in position. Jacob will take Julie in Ty's car. Andreas and Ty can create the diversion and maybe even walk out in the confusion with everyone else in the building."

"We'll set off the fire alarms," said Ty. He had packed up the camera equipment and handed the last memory chip from the camera to Josh.

"What about you? Where are you going?" asked Andreas.

Josh strapped his backpack on tight and pulled on his knit cap. "I'm heading for the nearest TV station on foot. Everybody ready?" He looked around the room, hand on the doorknob. There was no fear, only excitement and anticipation. Julie was zipping up a leather jacket with gloved hands. "Let's roll!"

Minutes later, Forman had established telephone contact with the front desk and was telling them to sit tight. He was getting information about the people he was after and the layout of the hotel. There was no basement or egress below the first floor. He knew about all the exits, and they were covered. Then he heard the sirens. "What the hell?" he shouted.

Liam smiled. "It's a party now, boys," he said to the two agents, who were not at all amused.

"Control, this is Burkhardt. We have Buffalo Fire Department over here, and I see patrol cars through the trees in back."

"Burkhardt stop BFD; they can't come in here," Forman barked into his handset.

Fisk chuckled. "Sir, those firemen would love to run over a few government vehicles, maybe agents too. They're serious!"

In the confusion of the fire truck's arrival, Burkhardt's backup agents had stopped in their tracks to see what was going on, and Julius attempted to slowly ease back into the driver's seat of his car through the still-open car door.

As Burkhardt turned around, motioning for the fire trucks to stop, Julius quickly started his engine with the driver's side door still open and gunned the engine. Burkhardt's men were running toward him and shouting.

Forman looked on in disbelief at the chaos. Everyone was looking toward the activity at the entrance to the parking lot. At the front of the hotel, despite the hotel manager's attempts to stop them, guests were pouring out into the covered entrance and the road that went past it. A lone figure emerged at the rear of the building in a blue FBI windbreaker and baseball cap.

Julius jumped the curb and tried to continue, but before he could drop down off the curb beyond the fire truck that was sounding its air horn, the backup agents had trapped him. He raised his hands and slowly stood up as the agents converged and took him to the ground.

"Fisk, how many agents do we have here?" Forman imagined his career slowly fading away like the fog coming in off Lake Erie.

"Twenty."

Forman shook his head. "You two handle the guests. Check them all. Commandeer some locals if you need to." He walked in the direction of the parking lot entrance and asked on his radio, "Burkhardt, who is your subject?"

"Julius Green, Ph.D. He's in custody now." As he answered, Burkhardt looked over at Julius being put in the back of a BPD patrol car, then jumped suddenly to the side as the firetruck sped past him as if oblivious, air horn sounding and sirens blaring.

Ty and Andreas had waited in the line of trees bordering the hotel property and walked out behind a patrol car while its driver took a sip of coffee. "Phew!" Andreas sighed as they ducked behind a restaurant.

"We're not out of it yet," said Ty. "We need to find transportation out of here. And I'm not feeling good about rental cars or cell phones right now."

"What about a bus?" Andreas suggested. He was looking toward a line of city busses traveling west about two blocks away.

Jacob and Julie had split off from Ty and the others in the trees and were already on the road in Ty's truck. Josh ditched the FBI garb in a dumpster and headed for downtown. He knew there were several stations only a few blocks away, but it was late, and he didn't want to wait for the late news. That would give the feds plenty of time to track him. If it was going to be that late, he would need to stay hidden even from the TV station staff. If the NSA were intelligent and resourceful enough, they would already have that angle covered. But based on the way things were going down at the hotel, he surmised that they were scrambling. Still, if he gave them the three hours between news shows, they would only get closer to catching him. Josh broke into a run through the long shadows of downtown as the sun crept lower in the sky.

CHAPTER FORTY-SIX

PUBLIC

Green Eggs & Ham Restaurant, Springfield, MA. 8:30a.m. Josh, Ty, Andreas, and John Thompson sat around a large round table. They were all laughing at something Thompson had just said. Some of them were still finishing their breakfast and asking for more coffee. Some had turned their chairs, and all faced a TV mounted in one corner of the restaurant. An advertisement ended, and a news program came on. Ty got everybody's attention. "Hey, hey, they're back. Check it out!"

It was the bottom of the hour, and they were recapping the top stories.

"The country is in shock today to find that a woman survived the attacks of September 11, 2001," the news anchor began. "Josh Aiden, the maker of the 9/11 conspiracy film *Freefall*, claims to have found and interviewed Julie Foley, a member of the crew of American Airlines flight 11, who has been presumed dead for over ten years. Our Terrence Pool spoke with Aiden last night."

As they showed the video of the interview with Josh, the whole table cheered, even the waitress joined in, raising her carafe of coffee in celebration. Then they got quiet, trying to listen to the interview.

"Not only do we have incontrovertible proof that there were conspirators in our government," Josh said to the reporter, "we know they are still in our government and were trying to prevent this from getting out."

The interviewer toughened up. "Your films have come under criticism for lack of objectivity and assumptions based on evidence that is vague at best. How do you answer the inevitable criticism that will come in light of your new film?"

"There is nothing vague about a flesh-and-blood human being that is alive and well. This person has assured us that in addition to appearing in our film, she will be available to news outlets that want to see for themselves that she is who we say she is."

"We certainly will give her the opportunity, Josh. Have you spoken with government officials about any of this? If what you are claiming is true, it surely means the investigation into 9/11 will have to be re-opened."

"I'm telling them right now…" He paused, looking into the camera. "No more secrets. It is time for the whole truth to come out!"

"Hey, look who's back!" Ty shouted. "Flo, bring some coffee for this ex-con here."

Julius walked into the door, waving his hands as if to say, "Free at last!" Everyone got up and hugged him or shook his hand.

"Have you seen this?" asked Ty, pointing at the TV.

"Heard it on the radio on the way over," Julius said, seated, turning to nod thanks to the smiling waitress.

"Well, you've had quite an exciting week for a psychologist. Might be a good topic for your next book."

"Book, hell! How about a lawsuit! They kept me there overnight for nothing, and my wife needs a new car." Everyone laughed as the celebration continued.

CHAPTER FORTY-SEVEN

WE CONTINUE

oston, Back Bay Amtrak station. Jacob and Julie walked along the platform. Across the tracks, the station was packed with commuters coming off the inbound trains. Jacob shoved his hands into his jacket, thinking this is the kind of cold that makes Bostonians feel at home. Like the summer heat, it is always more palatable when it is dry. For the first time, he noticed that Julie had a slight smile on her face and seemed relaxed. "Staying away from airplanes?" he asked as she stopped and stamped her feet against the cold.

Julie smiled, rolling her eyes toward the steaming train. "No. I love to fly, and I look forward to traveling again. Just thought I would try something different this time." She looked into Jacob's eyes and then looked down.

"So, what comes next?" he asked.

"Once I get to Arkansas, I need to take some time and reconcile this with the people closest to me," she said, a cloud of sadness crossing her face briefly. "I need to make sure I am healthy." The smile was coming back, revealing the natural optimism that must have been part of her personality always, but buried in the ten years of psychological imprisonment she had experienced. He imagined she had been an excellent flight attendant.

"That sounds like a good plan. Think you'll ever make it to New York?"

Julie's smile widened at his sweetness. "Definitely. I am not sure what the future holds, exactly. But I'm not unique, Jacob. Everyone else that was on that flight ... I just hope some of them survived, and I need to help them if I can."

"I'm sure you can and will." Julie's train had arrived at the station.

"Good luck with the film, Jacob. And with everything else. I'll never be able to thank you enough for what you did for me. My life will never be the same again." She leaned over and kissed him on the cheek. "Bye." Then she stepped onto the train, waving to him before she turned to climb the steps.

"Bye," said Jacob. He watched her walk through the train car, looking for her seat. He caught glimpses of her jet black hair between the headrests and through the fogged windows of the train. Minutes later, the train engines revved, filling the station with powerful sound as it slowly backed out.

He still feared for her, hoping that the light of publicity would keep darker forces from pursuing her further and that she would find peace in Arkansas. Satisfied for the moment, once the train left the station, Jacob jumped up from the bench and jogged up the stairs to the street, taking two at a time. There was work to do.

NSA Headquarters, Fort Meade, Maryland. 10 pm. M stood at his desk, loading papers and books into a stand-up leather satchel. The room was dark but for a lingering lamp and the glow of the fake fireplace on one wall. As M's assistant entered with his overcoat and helped him on with it, M3 appeared, sleeves rolled up, tie loosened, and stood, waiting with his hands in his pockets. When the assistant had closed the door behind her, M went to turn off the fake fire and the lamp, leaving his satchel on his desk.

There was no need for M3 to state the question.

"It doesn't matter," answered M. "Almost no one believes it, even now. There will be an explanation." He paused for M3's benefit, grabbed his satchel from the desk, and put his hand on M3's shoulder as he walked by. "But that's not our problem." M walked toward the door.

"So what happens now?" M3 pleaded, still grieving.

M turned around, slightly surprised that this manager hadn't given up yet. "What happens now is we continue. Soon enough, there will be another event. Most people will put Big Wedding in the back of their minds. Until then, we still have work to do." M turned back toward the office door for the last time. "I'll see you on Monday." M's assistant was waiting outside the door to M's office to walk him to his car and had left the door open. M3 stood in the dark room facing the shaft of fluorescent light penetrating the darkness from the hallway outside.

ACKNOWLEDGMENTS

I would like to thank some of the people who made this book possible: my editors and proofreaders Rose Lipscomb, C. B. Moore, and Alexa B.; and my beta readers Henrietta Davis, Wendy McLean, Denise Templeton, and Robert Smith.